CANDLES
IN THE
CLOSET

Candles In the Closet. Copyright © 2007 by Vera Propp. All rights Reserved. No part of this book may be used or reproduced in any manner whatsoever except in the case of brief quotation embodied in critical articles and reviews, without the written consent of the author.

To order additional copies of this title, contact your local bookstore. The author may be contacted at the following address:
Bennett Rose Publishing
13 Marion Avenue
Albany, NY 12203-1815

Cover and Book Design by Melissa Mykal Batalin

Published by Bennett Rose Publishing.

Printed by The Troy Book Makers in Troy, NY
on recycled, acid-free paper.
www.thetroybookmakers.com

ISBN-13: 978-1-933994-14-7
ISBN-10: 1-933994-14-2

CANDLES IN THE CLOSET

By Vera W. Propp

Dedication

To Richard

Acknowledgements

In September of 1998 I had a major stroke which put me out of commission for six months. Shortly after, in 1999, my first book, *When The Soldiers Were Gone*, was published. Later that same year I began *Candles In The Closet*, but for many years it was in a disorganized state in my computer. Joan Seidman was the first one to help me achieve a coordinated first draft. My editor had retired by then, and despite many attempts, I could not find a willing publisher of this book. I asked a few young friends, Jennifer Liebschutz, Rebecca Liebschutz, and Eliana Wachs Cashman to read the manuscript, and they felt it was a compelling story. When I heard about The Troy Book Makers, I decided to proceed. I will let you the reader decide on the wisdom of that decision.

Rabbi Donald Cashman and Dvorah Heckelman reviewed the book for Judaic accuracy. My assistant Melissa Brown helped bring it to publishing readiness. I thank all these people for their help, and I thank my friend Jim Trelease of *The Reading Aloud Handbook* fame for his kind words.

Heartfelt gratitude goes to my college classmate, author, science education consultant, and friend of 52 years, Sheila Tobias of Tucson, Arizona, for her constant interest in and encouragement of this project.

Vera W. Propp
Albany, New York
April, 2007

Table of Contents

BONNIE'S STORY

3 �܍ 1. Visiting Grandma and Discovering a Secret

15 ✜ 2. The Secret of the Candlesticks

LUISA'S STORY

29 ✜ 3. Where's Felipe?

41 ✜ 4. A Marriage Is Arranged

55 ✜ 5. Moving and a Narrow Escape

67 ✜ 6. A Letter from Felipe

CLARA'S STORY

85 ✜ 7. Jorge Seeks Adventure

95 ✜ 8. The Special Day

109 ✖ 9. The Decision is Too Difficult
115 ✖ 10. The Padre is at the Door!

ANA'S STORY

129 ✖ 11. Trouble On the Plaza
147 ✖ 12. Noni Bonita is Very Sick
159 ✖ 13. A Death

EPILOGUE

169 ✖ I. Part One
199 ✖ II. Some Bad News
201 ✖ III. Mexico; The Present

CANDLES IN THE CLOSET

BONNIE'S STORY

New Mexico and Arizona, The Present

1

Visiting Grandma and Discovering a Secret

Bonnie stood in the middle of her grandmother's kitchen. She was puzzled. Where could Grandma be, Bonnie asked herself. She thought she had seen her grandmother walk into the kitchen to prepare dinner.

Bonnie had come into the kitchen to set the table and make a salad, as she did almost every evening during her two week visit in Albuquerque. However, when Bonnie got into the kitchen this evening no one was there.

Maybe Grandma went into the garden to pick some flowers for the table, she thought.

Bonnie went to the back door to look out. No one was in the garden.

As Bonnie turned around facing the empty kitchen again, her eyes caught a thin strip of light under the pantry door. Curious at this sight, she went to the pantry. She turned the knob and opened the door.

As soon as the door was slightly ajar, Bonnie knew she had found her grandmother because she heard her grandmother's voice. What was she saying? Bonnie couldn't understand any of the words. It wasn't English! But it didn't sound like Spanish either! She opened the door wider. She saw Grandma's back! It was a black silhouette in front of shimmering light, which covered the back wall and ceiling of the pantry. Grandma had a scarf over her hair. There were lit candles in front of her on a low shelf on the rear wall of the pantry. The sounds were clearer and louder now, but still not understandable: "Boruch atta... ah doe nigh, a-doe- nigh, ah-doe-nigh."

"Grandma! What are you doing?" Bonnie called, louder than she had intended.

Grandma whipped around. "Oh! Bonnie. You startled me, I didn't hear you come in. Come over here. I want to show you something. Watch what I do, but first close the door. Bonnie closed the pantry door, then joined her grandmother at the back of the pantry in front of the lit candles. Grandma spoke slowly in a tone barely above a whisper, "When you turn twelve this fall I will give these beautiful silver candlesticks to you. At that time I will ask you to take on the family obligation to light candles in these candlesticks in secret as the sun sets every Friday evening as a good luck omen, to protect your family from evil. I will also teach you what to say."

"Do I have to?" Bonnie asked.

"No. You don't have to, but, it would mean a lot to me if you did. Mothers have been passing these candlesticks down to their twelve year old daughters in our family for many generations in order to protect our family and keep it free of evil spirits. It is very important to me that the tradition continues. Respecting our ancestors and the family traditions they have faithfully observed gives each of us a special place in the world. That place has a meaning. When we know where we came from, we have a better idea of who we are and what our potential is."

"That's why the family rituals have always been important to me. I hope the rituals will one day become important to you so you will want to pass them down to your daughter when she is old enough to understand the responsibility. My mother kept a diary from the time she accepted the ritual of the candle lighting. In it she wrote her feelings about what she was learning and questions that she had. She gave me the diary on my twelfth birthday to prepare me to continue the family obligations, to keep the evil spirits far from our home."

"I never saw MY mother light the candles," said Bonnie, with her hands placed firmly on her hips.

"Yes, I know. Your mother was going through her 'hippie' stage when she was twelve and she refused to take the candlesticks and learn about our ancestors. She said she was more interested in improving the future than revering the past. Perhaps she regrets that decision now," said Grandma.

Then Bonnie said, "Well, I have never heard Mother mention the candlesticks and as far as I have noticed she doesn't do anything different on Fridays except make us eat fish. Other than that Fridays are the same as any other day except Sunday when we go to Mass."

Grandma continued, "Well, I hope I won't fail with you as I did with your mother. She is a good, devout and intelligent person. I'm sure the people in her law firm respect her abilities and I know she's also a very good wife and mother, but, she was stubborn about respecting the family traditions. I'm sorry to say, but that puts an extra burden on you, Bonnie, since you are my only granddaughter. My mother always told me that it was very important to respect our ancestors' traditions which must go down from mother to daughter. I'll let you read her diary. Your great grandmother, Ester, wrote in it about all the questions she had about the family traditions. I will give my mother's diary to you when you go back to Tucson next week. I'll bring the candlesticks when I come to Tucson this fall to celebrate your twelfth birthday. Then I'll show you the secret message engraved on them. I hope, by then, you will have had time to read some of the diary and will have made the decision to continue the family traditions."

⁜ ⁜ ⁜

On the bus back to Tucson, Bonnie took her great grandmother Ester's diary out of her tote bag and started to read. The diary was written in Spanish, but since Bonnie had been learning Spanish in school since fifth grade it was not too difficult for her.

2, Abril. 1913
Taxco, Mexico

Hoy celebré mis duodécimos cumpleaños.

Today I celebrated my twelfth birthday.

Mamacita gave me this beautiful journal. I will write in it every night before I go to bed. Mamacita told me many secrets today. They are very con-

fusing. I cannot talk about these secrets with anybody, so I will write them in this journal.

For a long time I have noticed that Mamacita went into the large closet next to the kitchen on Friday afternoons. She allowed no one to come with her and stayed there only a few minutes. Sometimes I could smell the hot wax of candles burning when I walked by the closet. But she kept the door locked and would never tell me what was in there.

Today Mamacita invited me into the closet with her. She took candles and a pair of beautiful, heavy candlesticks out of a cupboard. She put the candles in the candlesticks. Then, without a word, she lit a matchstick, handed it to me and motioned that I should light the candles. Then she repeated strange sounds with her eyes closed while she moved her arms around the flames. She said that she was bringing their warmth toward her body to keep the evil spirits far away from our home. She told me that it is important that she does this every Friday evening just as the sun is going down.

Then Mamacita put the lighted candles in the cupboard and we left the closet.

Now I know what Mamacita does in the closet. She told me that I must learn the ritual so I can protect my own home and family one day. I will write in this journal everything that I learn.

Mamacita told me not to worry about the candles in the cupboard. It is a special cupboard made of clay and will not burn.

I will write again tomorrow,
Ester

Bonnie closed the diary and thought to herself, this is just what Grandma was doing in her pantry. Bonnie looked out of the window of the bus. Then she thought, maybe I'll find out about another ritual if I read another entry. She opened the diary to the next entry.

6, Julio, 1913
Taxco, Mexico
My cousin Rebecca got married today at Santa Maria Iglesia. She looked

beautiful. I think the wedding Mass lasted more than an hour!

After the wedding there was a festive party in the church plaza. There was a lot of food, but mostly I danced with Diego! I'm getting to like Diego more and more. I think he likes me, too.

When the musicians were putting away their instruments, Mamacita whispered to me that we were going to a secret second wedding party at Rebecca's house. It is on my conscience that I had to tell a falsehood to my best friend, Carlotta, so she wouldn't know Rebecca was having another party, and I was invited! I couldn't tell Diego about it either. Only family members were invited. Too bad. It would be more fun if Carlotta and Diego were there.

I'll try to write again soon,
Ester

Well, thought Bonnie, more secrets. I'd better put this diary in a safe place as soon as I get home. Bonnie looked at her watch. I'll be on this bus for another hour. I might as well keep reading.

27, Septiembre 1913
Taxco, Mexico

I am very hungry. Mamacita said that since I celebrated my twelfth birthday last month, I could have no food today. I must stay home and fast like the grownups. Papa has been out of sorts all day. I'm sure it's because he's hungry!

Mamacita told me that Carlotta and Juanita and Diego must not know that I am fasting. It is a good thing that I am not with them today at school, but what excuse will I give the teacher tomorrow when I return?

I must wait for the sun to go down before I can eat again. Two more hours!

If I survive I'll write again.
Ester

10, Octubre 1913
Taxco, Mexico

I have been going into the closet to light candles with Mamacita every Friday night. Now I know what to say after I light them. I say, "Boruch atta a-do-nigh..." I don't know what these words mean, but Mamacita told me they must be said, or bad luck will come to everyone in our house. I don't want to risk that so I do exactly what she tells me to do.

Rosita saw me go into the closet last week. She wanted to know what I was doing there. Mamacita told me it's all right to make up a lie to tell Rosita, because it would be worse if she knew the truth and told somebody. Why would that be worse? I hate lying to my little sister, but I must do what Mamacita tells me.

Ester

I'll read the rest when I get home, Bonnie thought as she put the diary back in her tote bag.

2

The Secret of the Candlesticks

(Bonnie Writes a Letter to Family Members)

Bonnie knocked on the guest room door. This was the room her grandmother always stayed in when she was visiting Bonnie's home in Tucson.

"Come in, Bonnie, I've been waiting for you," said Grandma.

Her grandmother was sitting in the rocking chair by the window. Another chair was pulled up beside her. On Grandma's lap was a long package wrapped in white cloth.

"Are those the candlesticks?" asked Bonnie as she sat down in the chair near her grandmother.

"Yes, Bonnie, I brought them with me just as I promised. Now you can see the secret that I told you about this summer. Turn them upside down. What do you see engraved on the bottom?"

"This one says 'España, 1492'" said Bonnie. "I know España means Spain."

"Yes, Bonnie, you're right! The candlesticks came from Spain."

"Wow! 1492! That's the year that Columbus sailed to America from Spain. Do you think the candlesticks were on one of his boats?"

"That I don't know, but maybe the date is important! Check out your history books. Maybe you will find something else important that happened in Spain in 1492," said Grandma. "What does the other candlestick say?"

Bonnie turned the other one over. "It says, 'Luisa y Tomás.' Who were they?" she asked.

"They must have been our early ancestors, perhaps the original owners of the candlesticks. My mother told me that these are the candlesticks that have been passed down through the generations in our family."

"Did she tell you any thing more about Luisa and Tomás? How could we find out how their candlesticks got to you in Albuquerque 500 years after Luisa and Tomás had them?"

"I'm sorry, Bonnie, I don't know anything about Luisa and Tomás. All I know is what is in my mother's diary. She doesn't even mention them. I always wondered why not. That could be YOUR challenge. Try to trace our family back as far as you can. Maybe you'll discover something about Tomás and Luisa."

"I'd like to do it!" said Bonnie, "but frankly, I have no idea where to begin. Perhaps the Internet can help! I've heard that there are genealogy programs."

Grandma shook her head. "I don't know anything about the Internet, but you go ahead and try. Just let me know what I can do to help you. I'll give you the names and addresses of all our relatives that I know about. Maybe each one has a little information that you could piece together and come up with something significant. It will be very interesting to me to see what you do come up with."

"Thanks, Grandma, I guess contacting the relatives is a good way to start. I'll try that."

The first thing Bonnie did when she got back to her own room was to draft a letter to send to all the people on Grandma's list.

Dear-------.
You have never met me, but we are related. My name is Bonnie Lopez. My mother is Janna Lopez, My grandmother is Sofia Sanchez. My great grandmother was Ester Rodriguez. According to my grandmother, Ester is your relative, also. I am twelve years old. My birthday was last week. My grandmother gave me some very old candlesticks that she wants me to light on Friday nights in secret (She said I

could tell family members). The candlesticks have some information engraved on the bottom. They are from Spain in the year 1492. They belonged to Tomás and Luisa. Have you heard of Tomás and Luisa? Please write and let me know if you have ever heard of them. I am also interested in knowing the names of all your ancestors and whether any of them lit candles or did other rituals in secret to keep evil spirits away. I realize these are very personal questions and you might not feel comfortable giving out family secrets, but since we are of the same ancestry, I think it would be all right. I'll pass on to you whatever I find out from other members of the family. Maybe I'll discover something really interesting. Please write if you have any useful information.

Sincerely,
Bonnie Lopez
6842 North Campbell Ave.
Tucson, Arizona 85719

Bonnie sent this letter to all the first, second and third cousins, and aunts and uncles on the list that her grandmother had given to her. For two weeks she heard nothing, then, one day a letter from San Francisco arrived.

Dear Bonnie,
Thanks for writing, cousin! I wonder why we've never met. You ask some interesting questions. Unfortunately I don't have many answers. I never heard of Tomás and Luisa.
I do know a little bit about candle lighting though. I followed my mother down to our cellar one Friday afternoon.(I had noticed before that she often "disappeared" on Friday afternoons.) Anyway when I got to the cellar I saw her standing in a far corner lighting candles and chanting something that I didn't understand. She told me that her mother had made her promise to do this every Friday to keep her home free of evil spirits. It must work because I've never seen an evil spirit. When she asked me to continue this tradition for

the safety of my family, I said, of course I would. I am fourteen and have been sneaking into the cellar to light the candles for about two years. My mother also told me that secrecy was very important. I should never tell anyone that I was lighting candles at sunset on Fridays. Someone might be killed if anyone found out. It was easy enough to keep it secret, so you are the very first person I have ever told! I trust you not to kill me or anyone in my family. I would love to see the silver candlesticks from Spain. (I use some very nice porcelain candlesticks from Sedona, New Mexico, that my mother brought back from a trip there about ten years ago.) Does your family do other secret rituals? You mentioned the secret candle lighting to me first so I assumed it would be OK to tell you about it. Now I will tell you another secret tradition of our family. When I visited my great aunt Laura in L.A. last year I noticed an urn next to her front door. Whenever she passed it going in or out she touched it near its base then kissed her fingers. She told me that an ancestor made the urn and she had placed something in the clay near the base which would protect all those in the house if they kissed it when ever they passed by. I would love to see the silver candlesticks from Spain. Do you ever get up to San Francisco? Perhaps we could plan a meeting. You could bring the silver candlesticks with you, and we could drive down to L.A. and I would get to show you the urn. Keep in touch, Bonnie

I hope we can meet soon!

Yours truly,
Margarita Gonzalez
1494 Sixth Ave.
San Francisco, California 94122

Two weeks later, Bonnie received another letter from Los Angeles.

Dear Bonnie,
It was lovely hearing from you. I was familiar with your name and that of your mother and grandmother. But for some reason the California branch of our extended family has not had

much personal contact with you folks in Arizona and New Mexico. I think it's really a shame! Perhaps your letters will change that. I know my great niece Margarita would like to meet you and bring you here to L.A. for a visit. I would love that. Margarita told me that she mentioned my urn to you. I can tell you a little more about the urn, but, also I want to tell you what I know about Luisa. The urn was a gift to me from my grandmother, Ana Colon. She told me it had been made by her great grandmother, Bonita Sanchez. Bonita was an artist I think. According to my grandmother, Ana, before Bonita died she designed her own gravestone. She also told me that the name of our oldest ancestor in Mexico was Luisa.

I went to the family cemetery in Taxco, Mexico years ago when my mother was buried. While I was there I looked for Bonita's gravestone. It was very beautiful and unique. It was covered from top to bottom with etched flowers, but, it had no cross. I wondered why the padre would allow a gravestone without a cross on it in the church graveyard. Perhaps Bonita was an unusually dedicated member of the church, so he thought she should have whatever she wanted on her gravestone.

At that time I also looked for Luisa's headstone. I found a circle of small, very old headstones standing at different angles in the ground. Most of the writing on them had eroded to the point where it was not legible. But I did find one on which I could make out an "L." Feeling around that letter with my fingertips and using my imagination I thought I could make out the word "Luisa."

Love to you, Bonnie. I hope to meet you here in L.A. soon.
Great Aunt Laura Perez
8121 Creighton Ave.
Los Angeles, California 90045

Then a letter came from San Diego.

Dear Bonnie,
Thanks for writing, cuz. I don't know why we've never met. I'm twelve, too! But I'm different from you and my

cousin, Margarita. When my mother asked me to do the secret candle lighting I said, "No way! It sounds too weird! I don't believe in evil spirits."

So I can't be of much help to you. I never heard of Luisa or Tomás, but I would like to meet you. If you're ever in the San Diego area please give me a call. Also, if you find out anything really interesting about our family, I'd like to know about it. Thanks for writing.

Sincerely,

*Carmen Nunez
6655 Roca Dr.
San Diego, California 92128*

LUISA'S STORY

Palos, Spain, August, 1492

3

Where's Felipe?

"Luisa, come away from the window. You're not a servant girl!"

"Oh what does it matter, Mamacita? Everyone at the port is too busy loading the Pinta, the Nina and the Santa Maria to notice me behind the shutters. All the men and boys of Palos are out there hoping to get a glimpse of the great man, Capitan Cristobal Colon. They are not looking in this direction. There he is! He's talking to the governor! I wonder what they are saying."

Luisa pressed closer to the window. "Just think what riches he may find. He may come back with gold and silver and many jewels. I wish I could go with him."

"Don't talk foolishness, Luisa. Where do you get such ideas? Come away from the window. If your father saw you there he would not let you out of your room for a month! Felipe will tell you all that is happening, if you must know."

"Yes, I must know! I will make Felipe describe everything he has seen! I hope he comes home soon."

Mother sounded exasperated,"Enough of ships and Capitan Colon! It's time you finished embroidering that handkerchief. Come here and show me what you've done so far. Did you finish the border, yet? You're already twelve years old and you haven't even started embroidering the bedding for your dowery! Your father asks me everyday if you've started your pillowcases."

Luisa reluctantly turned away from the window. She straightened her lace cap, which had become dislodged as she pressed her face against the shutters. She flipped her long black curls to the back and walked sedately back to her chair. She picked up the partially embroidered handkerchief lying there and took the handiwork over to her mother.

"Your stitches are nice and even." Mother smiled, then turned the handkerchief over. The smile faded. "What is this? What a tangle of threads. This mess must come out before you can go on. What am I going to do with you? How will we find a husband for you? The wrong side must look neat, too. I'll rip it out, then you must try again. The handkerchief must be perfect, front AND back, before you can start on the pillowcases."

Luisa sat down next to her mother as tears welled up in her eyes. "Felipe is outside with all the excitement. All I'm allowed to do is sit here and embroider. I hate embroidering! Why couldn't I have been born a boy?"

Mother wiped the tears from Luisa's eyes with her own handkerchief and looked at her sympathetically for a minute. She kissed her cheek, then handed Luisa's handkerchief back to her. "Now, start again, niña, and keep your stitches small and neat on the back as well as on the front. I think you *are* improving."

"I'll never embroider as well as you do," Luisa said, sniffling. "I am trying, but at the same time I'm always thinking that I'd rather be doing something else. Embroidery seems so useless. Why not sleep on plain pillowcases?"

"You'd probably be surprised to know that I felt the same way you do when I was your age," Mother sighed. She put down her embroidery and gazed towards the window. "But I got used to following my mother's example. I knew my parents wanted what was best for me. They told me that it was important to live modestly so that a good family would choose me as the wife for their son. Your father has been a decent husband and a loving parent to you and Felipe. When you are married to a good man you will feel proud that you can make his household run smoothly so he can conduct his affairs of business without the worries of the home. And when you have children you must care for them and be a good example to them.

These are the things that make a woman happy."

"Ouch!" Luisa put her finger in her mouth. "I'm not good at this. I'm good at reading and I like doing figures. I could help my husband in other ways. I could help him with his accounts."

"Enough! That is not woman's work! I don't want to hear anymore of it. No self-respecting husband wants a woman interfering with his business dealings. Where do you get these ideas?"

"Sometimes they just spring into my head, especially when I prick my finger with the embroidery needle."

"Well, let them spring right back out of your head and use your thimble! Now stay away from the windows, I have to go see how the servants are doing with the supper preparations."

"Mother, now that we're Catholics will we be lighting the Sabbath candles tonight? I didn't see the silver candlesticks on the table."

"No, Luisa. We will not be lighting candles anymore. I gave the candlesticks away to be melted down with the Hannukah menorah and the Mezuza that was on the door. The Friday night candle lighting is for Jews. We are not Jews anymore. We don't want those Jewish symbols in our house."

"But, why? Tell me again. Why are we Catholics now?"

"Look, the sun is going down, I must go! I'll explain it to you another time. Where is Felipe? Did you hear him come in? Where is your father?"

Mother put her embroidery away and quickly left the room. Luisa laid her handkerchief aside and went back to the window. Large gas lanterns lit the port now and outlined the shapes of the ships there. Luisa could see long black shadows of sailors pushing heavy barrels up the gangplanks. The scraping sounds of the rolling barrels and excited commands to the workmen penetrated the night air as they had all afternoon. Live pigs and chickens were making protesting sounds as they, too, were being taken up the gangplanks. The loading would continue until everything was on board. Father had said that Capitan Colon and his crews would also board tonight and sleep on the ships. The Nina, the Pinta and the Santa Maria would set sail at first light.

Luisa wondered how she would ever be able to sleep with all this activity going on just outside her window knowing that the ships might pull out of port before she woke up the next day. The oil lamps on the chandelier in the eating room had been lit. Luisa heard the voices of the servants in the kitchen, but where was her mother? Where were her father and brother?

She started up the stairs to see if Felipe had come home. She wanted him to tell her all that he had seen at the port this afternoon. Had he seen Cristobal Colon? As Luisa walked up the stairs, carrying her candle to light her way she was struck by the heat of the upstairs on this second day of August. Her brother's room was dark, but she smelled melting candle wax and then noticed a flickering light under the door of the large closet in the hall. She tiptoed near the door and pressed her ear against it. Luisa could hear her mother's voice whispering the prayer for welcoming the Sabbath and she smelled the melting candle "Baruch atta adonai elohenu melech ha'olam, asher kide shono bemits vo sav vitsivanu l'ha dlig neer shel Shabbat. Praised be thou, O Lord our God, who sanctified us by thy laws and has commanded us to light the Sabbath lights."

Luisa suddenly felt cold. Had her mother lied to her about melting down the silver candlesticks? Why was she lighting the Sabbath candles in the closet? What if the servants heard her or saw the flickering light? Would they tell Queen Isabel that Mother was still practicing Jewish rituals? Maybe Felipe could explain it to her; after all, he had had his Bar Mitzvah last year. Surely he would have come home by now!

Luisa soundlessly backed away from the closet door and tiptoed back down the steps.

"Hello, Luisa, my beauty! What have you been doing today?"

It was Father. He was sitting in the eating room. "Come here and give me a kiss."

Father was a big man with a deep voice that sometimes scared Luisa, but she obediently walked over to him and kissed his bearded cheek. "I've been embroidering, Father," she said softly.

"Good, good. It is time that we find a good husband for you. I've been talking to Jose Martinez, his son..."

"Fernando," Mother interrupted as she quickly came down the stairs. "I'm glad you're home. Have you seen Felipe? He hasn't come home yet. Where could he be?"

"Don't worry, Francisca, I saw him talking to my brother Solomon at the port. Maybe he went home with Solomon for the evening meal. He's fourteen now. A young man. Don't treat him like a baby."

"I know I have to let him grow up, but times are so uncertain now. Queen Isabel's spies are everywhere. Maybe he'll say something foolish."

Luisa laughed, "I think everything he says is foolish. Why would Queen Isabel care?"

"Hush, Luisa. Go tell Maria we are ready for our supper." Mother was not laughing.

✄ ✄ ✄

Maria came in with platters piled high with fish, vegetables and sweets and returned when the three had finished eating to take the empty platters out. No one talked about Felipe while Maria was in the room. After the meal Mother urged Father to go to his brother Solomon's house so he could walk home with Felipe. Father and Mother both kissed Luisa and she went upstairs to her room. It was 10:30. She undressed and went right to bed so she could wake up early enough to watch Capitan Colon and his ships set sail early in the morning.

✄ ✄ ✄

Bright sunlight streaked through the slats of the shutters and woke Luisa. Because of the heat she had left her shutters partially open. She ran to her window and opened them wider. No ships were in the port! Luisa squinted against the sun and saw the Pinta, the Nina and the Santa Maria out in the middle of the sea, far in the distance. Their big sails were puffed out and the ships appeared to be getting smaller and smaller. Luisa was angry at herself for sleeping so late. She dressed quickly and went downstairs. Mother was at the table weeping silently. Father was holding her hand. They looked up when Luisa walked into the room.

"Your brother and uncle sailed on the Santa Maria." Father said.

4

A Marriage Is Arranged

Luisa ran to the window. She couldn't believe that Felipe was actually sailing on the Santa Maria! How could she cross that huge span of water to be with him? Of course, there was no way! She wanted to share with her brother the adventure of sailing to the Indies with Capitan Christobal Colon! What a silly thought. Girls didn't have adventures!

"Luisa!" Her father's voice, loud and gruff, called out from the eating room. "Come away from that window immediately. Someone will see you. Where is your modesty? You can't see Felipe anyway, the ships are almost to the other side of the sea!"

Her mother gently pulled Luisa away from the window. "Come sit down, Luisa. We have some serious matters to discuss with you."

Mother's arm around Luisa's waist guided her to the table where her father was sitting. The smell of bread baking and fish frying came from beyond the kitchen door. But Luisa was not hungry. Her great disappointment about having missed the launching of the ships and her envy of Felipe's adventure had completely taken away her appetite. She sat down across from her father and lowered her eyes, as she had been taught.

"Luisa. I have some important news to tell you. Look at me."

"Yes, Papa." Luisa looked into his eyes. They appeared to be even more stormy and black than usual.

"Luisa, Felipe made the decision to sail on that ship without our knowledge. I found out last night when I went to my brother Solomon's house. Your cousin, Juan, had watched Solomon and Felipe push heavy barrels up the gangplank onto the Santa Maria and then he waited for them to come off the ship. They never did. When the gangplank was pulled up, Juan ran home to tell his mother. Her eyes were still red from crying when I got there, but there was nothing any of us could do."

"But why was she crying, Papa? Surely Tio Solomon and Felipe will return with wonderful tales of their adventures."

"IF they return! Queen Isabel would not want Jews to be part of an important trip of a Spanish discovery. For her, everything having to do with Spain must be Roman Catholic."

"But I thought we are all Catholics now." Luisa looked from her father to her mother. "Isn't that so?"

"Yes, Luisa, we have all converted. But....in our hearts....in our minds....in secret...we will always be Jews." Her father's eyes softened as he uttered these words.

"What will happen to Tio Solomon and Felipe if Capitan Colon finds out that they are Jewish in their hearts, Papa?"

"We don't know what he will do, but when the Palos authorities find out that Solomon and Felipe are missing, they will soon figure out that they left on one of Colon's ships. The authorities will then become suspicious of the rest of the family. Things might become very dangerous for us. In fact..." he stopped and looked at Luisa's mother with pleading eyes, as if saying, help me.

"Luisa, listen carefully to what your father is telling you!" Luisa's mother was alternating between wringing her hands and smoothing the front of her dress with them. Luisa had never seen her look so nervous.

"What is it, Papa, go on. What do you want to tell me?"

"Luisa, in two weeks you will be married! There is no other way!"

"What did you say? Married? Me? Why must I marry? Who will I marry? What do **I** have to do with Felipe's voyage?" Luisa pushed her heavy chair back, knocking it over, and stood up.

She glared first at her father, then at her mother. This cannot be true, she thought!

My brother is sailing across the ocean and I must marry! No! I won't do it! It is not fair!

She ran around the table and knelt down in front of her mother, pressing her hands together as if in prayer, "Mamacita, help me! I beg you to help me! I can't marry yet. I'm not ready."

Her mother cradled Luisa's hot face in her hands. "You must, Luisita. Do you think this decision was easy for us? Your father and I have been sitting right here talking all night! We agree that it is the only way."

Luisa's father interrupted, "Stand up, Luisa. You must be sensible. Queen Isabel's spies are everywhere, watching everything your mother and I do. They will become even more suspicious that we are not true believers in Catholicism because of what Felipe did. They will think he ran away to escape Isabel's priests. We want YOU to be safe. The only way you will be safe is to become part of another family. I went early this morning to see my friend Jose Martinez."

Luisa was still on her knees, her head in her mother's lap. Her father got up and paced around the table, puffing on his big pipe. "Jose Martinez is a good friend, Luisa. He understands our situation and wants to help us. He agreed to allow the marriage between you and his son, Tomás, even before all the details of the dowry are settled. Señora Martinez will help you finish embroidering your bedding."

"How can you talk of embroidery?" Luisa cried out. "I hope there is more to my life than embroidery!"

Her mother took Luisa's hands into her trembling ones and gently pulled her up. She looked into Luisa's eyes. "Señor and Señora Martinez have been very kind, Luisa. You must respect them just as if they were your own parents. They, too, have converted and they always behave like good Catholics. No one suspects them of Jewish acts, so you will be safe with them. You must obey your husband, also. You must do whatever he asks of you. We pray for you to have a very long life filled with happiness and love. That is why we have made this decision."

Luisa scanned her mother's worried face. She swallowed hard and squeezed her eyes shut to keep the tears from spilling out. "Yes, Mama," she whispered.

"Her father walked over and stood behind Luisa. He put his hands on her shoulders and kissed the top of her black curls. Talking to the back of her head, he said in a low voice, "Tomás saw you, Luisa, one day when you were in our garden. He had brought some papers to me from his father and happened to notice you reading there. Of course he didn't say anything to me, but he did mention something to his father when he returned home. He must have liked what he saw, Luisa, because he agreed immediately when his father mentioned this marriage to him."

Luisa whipped around to face her father, tears streaming down her face, "But Father, I've never seen HIM. What does HE look like? What if **I** DON'T like what **I** see on my wedding day? What if I DON'T LIKE HIM?"

"What does it matter, Luisa?" her father said, wiping her tears with the back of his hand. "With Tomás and his family you will be protected. In these times that is all that matters! We Jews must stay alive! Now call Maria. I am hungry for my morning meal. Afterwards you must help your mother with the wedding preparations. I will go talk to Padre Josefo."

✂   ✂   ✂

On their wedding day Luisa and Tomás knelt in front of Padre Josefo at Santa Teresa Iglesia. Luisa kept her eyes lowered while the priest read the marriage rites. All she had seen of Tomás so far were his large, tanned hands holding hers. But when it was time for them each to repeat their vows, Luisa looked up, for the first time, into Tomás' face through her heavily embroidered veil. She breathed a soundless sigh of relief. He doesn't look too bad, she thought, for someone who is already 30 years old.

"Si," they whispered their replies to the priest's questions.

The nave of the old church was filled with flowers, friends and relatives of the two families witnessing the beauty and solemnity of the nuptial mass. Afterwards they went to a feast at the Lopez home.

The food was abundant. Fresh fruit, roasted meats, nuts, cake and wine. The guests talked and laughed while they ate. The servants bustled around keeping the platters filled.

Luisa sat on a banquette with her mother and the other women, including Señora Martinez, Tomás' mother. Mostly, she kept her eyes lowered, but occasionally she peeked across the room at her new husband. He was easy to pick out, in his white wedding suit, from the other men of his age. He's definitely the best of that group, Luisa thought. What a nice laugh he has... "Luisa, did you get something to eat?" her mother asked quite loudly, shaking her shoulder.

"What mother? What did you say?"

"Luisa! Did you eat? I've asked you three times and you don't answer!"

"I'm sorry, Mamacita, I didn't hear you. Yes, I ate some fruit and cake. It was delicious."

The women fluttered their fans in front of their lips, trying to hide their smiles.

"Luisa," Tomás' mother said, "your father's servants made six trips to our house yesterday with your trunks. We can hardly walk upstairs without falling over one of them. You must start unpacking as soon as possible!" Luisa would be moving to the Martinez home right after the festivities that night.

Luisa's mother answered quickly, "Luisa will do whatever you say Señora Martinez. I know Luisa will not make difficulties for you or your servants. Is that not so, Luisa?" Luisa's mother turned to look at her.

"I hope you will be happy to have me in your house, Señora Martinez." That was all Luisa could say. She felt shy around this woman, her new mother-in-law.

As it became dark the guests started to leave. Only the close relatives stayed. They said that they wanted to drink a last cup of wine to toast their newly linked families.

The servants took the empty platters to the kitchen. Señora Lopez thanked them for their extra work and told them to take the night off. They could leave as soon as the kitchen was back in order and they had pulled the heavy window drapes closed in the main rooms and lit the oil lamps.

Señor Lopez gave each servant a gold coin and told them to be sure to return in time to prepare his morning meal.

When the last servant had left, Luisa's father went out, too. Her mother went up the stairs, returning a few minutes later with the silver candlesticks from the closet in the hallway and fresh candles. She placed them on the table in the center of the eating room.

The room grew silent as those remaining heard the heavy wooden front door creak open again. In a moment, Luisa's father entered the room with a small man. The man had a grey beard. When he removed his hat, Luisa could see that under it he wore a little, black skull cap. He was carrying what looked like four sticks from brooms.

"Luisa, Tomás come to the table," Señor Lopez implored.

"This is Rabbi Itzak. Now you two will **really** be married. But hurry. There is not much time; someone might come!"

Luisa's mother lit the candles in the beautiful silver candlesticks. Her father draped his white, silk prayer shawl over the four broomsticks. He asked three of Luisa's cousins to each hold up one stick while he held up the fourth. Then he beckoned to Luisa and Tomás to stand in front of the rabbi, under the canopy that was created by the upright sticks and cloth. This solemn group cast long shadows onto the walls of the room.

Tomás took Luisa's hand into his again. The rabbi read the brief Hebrew wedding ceremony. When he had finished, the couple and their witnesses signed the Katubah, the Jewish marriage contract. Then Tomás threw a crystal wine glass into the air. When it fell to the tiled floor it shattered into many pieces. He kissed his new bride on the forehead. Luisa heard "Mazel Tov", "Good

Luck", as one by one the relatives kissed her on the cheek.

Then quickly the candles were snuffed out, the shawl was folded up and the broomsticks were returned to the rabbi. He and the relatives left the house singly or in couples so not to arouse any suspicions.

At last only Luisa and Tomás and Luisa's parents remained.

"You must take these with you, Luisa." Her mother pressed the silver candlesticks into Luisa's hands. "No one will search your trunks in your new home. When times are safer for Jews, light them as you used to see me light them to welcome the Sabbath, the most holy of our holidays."

"I will, Mama. I wish you could visit me at the Martinez home."

"It is too dangerous, Luisa. You must not come here either. We will say 'goodbye' now. We pray that we will all be able to leave Spain soon. Perhaps Felipe will find a place in the Indies, far away from Queen Isabel, where we can be together and happy again. We can only hope and pray that it will happen soon."

Luisa gave each of her parents a kiss and a long hug. All their tears had been shed during the last two weeks whenever they had spoken of this moment of parting. Luisa swallowed hard.

Tomás placed her cloak over her shoulders and took Luisa's hand. With her free arm she clutched the silver candlesticks next to her heart, under her cloak. And with a long look backward Luisa left her childhood home, perhaps forever.

5

Moving and a Narrow Escape

Luisa felt like a little sister in the Martinez household. Everyday she sat next to Señora Martinez and embroidered the sheets, pillowcases and tablecloths that she would use in her own home one day.

"Your stitches are getting smaller and more even." Señora Martinez told Luisa one day after she had been there a few weeks. "I am very pleased with your improvement." Señora Martinez smiled and patted Luisa's hands.

"Thank you, Señora Martinez. I hope Tomás will be pleased, too." She was trying to be the good daughter-in-law and wife that her mother had asked her to be.

Tomás kissed her on the forehead as he left the house each day to go to business with his father. The men bought and sold gold, silver and jewels. Sometimes they had to travel to trade fairs a great distance away and were gone for two or three weeks at a time.

When Tomás and his father were away it was very quiet in the house. Señora Martinez kept busy with her embroidery and supervising the household tasks. Some afternoons she would exchange visits with her friends. Luisa excused herself from these visits whenever possible and went to her room or the garden to read or study mathematics and geography from Felipe's books, which she had brought with her. She liked to look at maps and tried to trace the route that Felipe and the Santa Maria might have sailed.

When Tomás was home, Luisa spent many hours walking hand in hand with him in the garden. They talked of many things.

"When you are tired of Felipe's books you can look at mine," Tomás told her. "You are not like my cousins, Sofia and Carolina. They have no interest in books."

"Thank you, Tomás. Your mother tells me I should spend less time reading, it might injure my eyes. But I think too much embroidery is also bad for the eyes and does nothing for the brain! Don't you agree?"

"Whatever makes you happy, Luisita, is what I want you to do. I will tell my mother not to interfere."

"No, Tomás. Do not say anything. She means well and does not bother me when I read. It is better that she does not hear any of my complaints. She is very good to me."

"She told me that she has come to love you, as you know I do, too, Luisa." He stopped walking and kissed her cheek. "I wish I could take you with me on some of my trips, but the roads are very dangerous. Bandits are everywhere. When Father and I stop at an inn we sleep in our clothes to be ready at a moment's notice for any mishap. It is too difficult for a woman to travel in these times. But I miss you when I'm away."

"And I, you, Tomás."

Luisa often saw Tomás' parents watching them from the vestibule when she and Tomás walked in the garden, but they rarely joined them.

It was during these walks that Luisa came to know how tender-hearted her husband was. He always brought bread crumbs with him to feed the birds.

Luisa was happy in the Martinez home. Everyone was very kind to her. It was only when she thought about her own parents and brother that she became melancholy.

"Tomás, what have you heard of Colon's voyage? Why do you think that Felipe didn't come back with him?" Luisa asked in their room one evening.

"You heard, Luisa, that only the Pinto and Nina came back. Perhaps Felipe stayed in the Indies because there was no space for him on those two ships. Perhaps he did not want to return to Spain. I did not hear his name mentioned when the list was read of those who died on the voyage."

"Then why doesn't he write to us?"

"I don't know, Luisa. Whenever I hear men talking about the voyage, I try to stand near to listen. I hope that I will hear Felipe's name mentioned. But I don't dare ask about him. I think you will hear from him soon."

Every Sunday the Martinez family went to Mass at Santa Teresa de Avila Iglesia. As Luisa walked by the candles there she remembered the warm glow the candles had had in her home on Friday nights when she was a child. She closed her eyes as she passed them remembering how her mother always had covered her eyes when lighting the Sabbath candles. But Luisa never used her mother's silver candlesticks. They were still deep in the trunk in which she had placed them on her wedding night.

One Friday evening Tomás was away and Luisa felt very lonely. She was alone in her room and decided to open the trunk just to look at the candlesticks lying there. It had been almost a year since she had heard the blessing over the candles that sanctified the Sabbath for Jews. Could she still remember it?

"Baruch Atah Adonai," she whispered into the trunk, "Elohenu...? What comes next?"

"Oh, dear, I can't remember anymore!" she said out loud just as, Julia, a servant girl came into her room to light the lamps.

"What don't you remember, señora? Can I get something for you?" Luisa liked Julia; she had always been very helpful to her. But she was afraid to trust any of the servants.

"Oh, no!" said Luisa looking up and closing the trunk lid quickly. "I was just trying to remember a poem my nurse taught me years ago when I was a child, but I have forgotten it."

How careless I've been, she thought. What if Julia heard me speak the Hebrew words! "Do you know the poem about the bird who flew in the window?" she asked the servant girl.

"No, señora, I don't, but I'll ask the other servants."

"That's all right, Julia. It's not important."

The servant left the room and Luisa locked her trunk vowing not to be so careless again.

She placed the key in an inside pocket of her cloak. She didn't want to endanger the Martinez household. But she did miss the Jewish customs she had grown up with. No one in the Martinez family ever mentioned their Jewish past, not even Tomás. Had they forgotten the Jewish rituals, Luisa wondered? Or were they just being extra cautious?

Just two nights earlier at the evening meal, Señor Martinez had told the family that he had seen new notices from Queen Isabel and King Fernando posted at the market place. They proclaimed that it was the duty of good servants to report any suspicious activities among the New Christians for whom they worked.

Every Sunday at Mass, Luisa, herself, heard the padre speak of the sin of Judaizing, performing Jewish rituals in secret. He ordered his parishioners to report to him any signs of Judaizing they saw or heard about.

No servant ever heard anything suspicious in the Martinez home, because nothing Jewish ever happened there. But what of her own parents? Hadn't she seen the glow of her mother's candles under the hall closet door and heard her praying there? Had the servants seen and heard her, too? What other Jewish rituals might her mother and father be observing in secret? Luisa wanted to beg them to stop when she saw her parents at Mass every Sunday, but she couldn't talk with them. Her parents usually sat in the last row, not up in front like the Martinez family. They looked away when Luisa tried to make eye contact with them.

Mama, look at me! Luisa would think. I love you. Be careful! Don't take chances. But there was no opportunity for her to say this to her mother.

Then one Sunday Luisa didn't see her parents at Mass. "Perhaps they were not feeling well today." Tomás tried to reassure her. The next week they were not there either.

"I'm worried, Tomás. I feel that something has happened to my parents. Can you ask about them?"

"Yes, Luisa. I'll do my best, but you know that I have to be careful. If I ask too many questions, the authorities will become suspicious of me, too. Then I can do nothing more."

"I understand, but find out what you can. I am so worried about my mamacita!"

Luisa did not want to walk in the garden that afternoon. She told the family that she was not feeling well and went to her room. As she lay on her bed she couldn't stop her tears. What if I never see them again? I couldn't bear that. I must remember to pray for my parents' safety everyday.

A knock on her door startled her. "Luisa, may I come in?" It was the voice of her father-in-law on the other side of the door.

She got off the bed, straightened her hair and sat down on the chair by the window to receive him. "Come in. You are welcome," she said.

Jose Martinez looked very serious as he strode into the room and sat down next to Luisa. Tomás walked in right after him and stood behind Luisa's chair. He rested his hands on her shoulders.

Jose Martinez cleared his throat. "Luisa, it is my duty to bring you sad news. I would give away a fortune in jewels if I could find a way to change what I have to tell you."

"What is it? Is it about my parents? Are they sick or in trouble?"

Jose Martinez took Luisa's hands in his. "It's worse, Luisa. Two weeks ago, after mass, your parents' neighbors reported to Father Josefo that your parents never went to the market on Saturdays and that your parents' cook had told their cook that your parents never ate pork. The padre reported this to Queen Isabel's soldiers. Last Sunday, the royal soldiers arrested your parents for Judaizing just as they were entering the iglesia. They are in prison still."

"In prison! Oh my poor mamacita! When can I see them? How can we get them out?" Luisa turned to Tomás. "Tomás, will you help me. I must go see them at once."

"Luisa, you must do nothing, or you will be in prison, too." Jose Martinez said gently. "Your parents knew this might happen after your brother Felipe went away. That is why they wanted your wedding so soon. You must stay away from them. You cannot even send them a note." Jose Martinez stood up. "I'll leave you two now. Tomás, you must explain again to your wife that she has to be sensible. Luisa, I'm very sorry. Your father was a much valued friend. Your parents are good people. These are terrible times in Spain." He left the room.

Luisa wiped the tears from her cheeks. She felt she had to do SOMETHING to help her parents. She was the only one they had. "What should I do, Tomás?"

"You can do nothing, Luisa. You must not put your life in danger. That is not what your parents would want."

"Tomás, please lock the door to our room."

He walked across the room and did what she asked.

Then Luisa took the key from her cloak, unlocked her trunk and reached in for the silver candlesticks. She clutched them close to her heart while she recited the one Hebrew prayer that she remembered, "Shema Yisroel, Adonai Elohenu, Adonai Echod, Hear O Israel, the Lord our God, the Lord is One." She kissed the candlesticks and returned them to the trunk and locked it again.

Luisa then walked to the window, sat down and picked up her embroidery. Tomás sat beside her. They watched the sun go down and did not talk.

A few weeks later Jose Martinez came home from his business and told Luisa that he had heard that her parents had died in prison. He didn't know any details.

Luisa went to her room. She did not go down for the evening meal. The next morning she went downstairs and joined the Martinez family in the eating room for breakfast. She kept her eyes lowered while she ate, although she knew the family would be too polite to mention how red and puffy they looked. No one spoke of her parents.

6

A Letter from Felipe

"Luisa, I have news, good news!" Tomás said as he burst into their bedroom one afternoon. Luisa was resting.

He bent over the bed and whispered in her ear, so the servants wouldn't hear, "Finally we have someplace to go. We can leave Spain." He kissed Luisa on the cheek. "I must get Mama and Papa, I'll be right back!"

A few minutes later he came back in the room with his parents. He closed the door.

"The good news is that King Juan of Portugal died last week. Manuel the First, his son, is the new king!" Tomás sounded very excited.

"Why is that good?" Luisa asked.

"Luisa," he said, still in a low voice, "King Manuel has released all the enslaved Jews in Portugal. He is allowing Jews to live freely in his country. We must pack up and go there at once while Portugal's borders are still open. We will not have to live in fear there."

Three years had passed since the death of Luisa's parents. *If only my parents had lived to see this day,* she thought, but she did not let her husband see her feelings of sadness. She showed him only her joy at leaving Spain. Queen Isabel was suspicious of all the New Christians. All those who were charged with Judaizing were put to a cruel death. Luisa knew that Spain was a very dangerous place for them to live.

The next day the whole Martinez household started packing and two weeks later they were on the road heading to Portugal. They took only what could fit onto two large carts pulled by horses. They went to Dagos, Portugal, where Jose Martinez had business associates. It took them a week to get there. The trip was hot and bumpy. Luisa felt sick the whole way, but did not complain.

"We will live with the gold seller, Fernando da Fima," said Jose Martinez," I have known him a long time. He will help us start our own little jewelry business in Dagos."

"I hope we can find our own house soon," Tomás told his father. "I have good news. Soon there will be a new little Martinez!"

Juanita was born to Luisa and Tomás a few months later. Luisa was fifteen years old.

✤   ✤   ✤

One day, as Luisa was sitting in the garden of their new little house with Juanita next to her in the baby carriage, a servant approached her.

"Señora Martinez, a sailor is at the front door. He asks if someone here has a brother named Felipe Lopez. What should I tell him?"

"Tell him 'yes'. Bring him to me immediately!"

A few minutes later the sailor was sitting across from Luisa and she was reading a note that he had given to her. It was the first news she had received from her brother, Felipe, since he left that early morning in August in the year 1492.

Tears streamed down Luisa's cheeks as she read the note.

"This note is dated November 12, 1492," Luisa wiped away her tears and looked at the sailor. "Today is June 3, 1495. Why did it take so long to get to me?"

"I don't know, señora. I received it from a friend a month ago and brought it here to Dagos when I came to visit my parents. A sailor I know heard that I was going to Dagos. The sailor had been carrying this note for a long time looking for your parents in Palos, Spain. Finally an old servant girl of your parents told him that they had died in prison and you lived in Dagos. The sailor asked me to try to find you here. I had only your name, but my parents were able to direct me to this house. They had heard that recent arrivals from Spain had moved here."

"I thank you and your parents. I have been awaiting this letter for a long time."

The sailor left and Luisa read the note again.

It was very short.

Dearest Family,

Forgive me for leaving Palos without telling you beforehand, but I only decided myself at the last minute, while the sailors were pulling up the gangplank. Colon was willing to take me and Tio Solomon with him if we helped load up the ship and promised to take our shifts on the night watch with the regular sailors. I will tell you all about the voyage when I see you again. What is important for you to know now is that Tio Solomon and I are staying on the island of Haiti, with some other Jews who were on the ship. We will build a synagogue. I pray for the day when we can be together again.

Your loving son and brother,
Felipe

When Tomás came home, Luisa showed him the note.

"Tomás, would it be possible for us to go to Haiti? Do you think we could find a ship to take us there?"

"Perhaps, Luisa. It would be quite an adventure for us and little Juanita. I have a little money saved up to pay a ship captain to take us to Haiti. Maybe it will be possible."

Then one day, a few weeks later, as the family sat around the table for the evening meal, Luisa's mother-in-law told them what she had heard at the marketplace that afternoon. "They say that King Manuel wants to marry." she told them.

"Has he picked out a bride?" Jose asked.

"Oh, yes," Señora Martinez answered. "They say he has chosen, Juana, the daughter of Queen Isabel and King Fernando."

First there was only silence then they all said, "Oh, no," almost in unison. Such a marriage would mean that they had not escaped Queen Isabel's cruel laws.

Tomás, himself, brought home the news the following day. "Queen Isabel has told King Manuel that he must expel all the Jews from Portugal before she will allow him to marry their daughter."

"Maybe you two and Juanita should go to Haiti now," said Jose, "I have heard of ships leaving Portugal, carrying wine and other cargo to Haiti and other islands near there."

"What about you and Mama? Where will you go, Papa?" Tomás asked.

"Many Jews are being allowed to enter Turkey. That would be an easier voyage for Mama and me. We are too old for a long sea voyage."

"But we have one year to decide," Jose added quickly. "King Manuel has decreed that the Jews can stay until December, 1497."

✣ ✣ ✣

A few months later a notice was distributed among all the Jews of Portugal instructing them that ships would be awaiting them at the port in Lisbon to take them wherever they wanted to go, on March 19, 1497, but only from the port of Lisbon and only on that day. The Martinez family packed up again. Luisa was pregnant for a second time, but she was feeling fine and very excited because they had heard about a cargo ship that was going to Haiti. Tomás had bargained with a representative of the captain. He would take Tomás, Luisa and Juanita if he was paid in advance. Tomás complied with his request. The captain said the ship would be loading at the port in Lisbon.

But when the Martinez family arrived at that port, along with twenty thousand other Jews, expecting to board ships, no ships were there.

"Where's the boat, Mama? I don't see a boat, Papa." Little Juanita was right. There were no ships in the port.

"They will come, Juanita," Luisa told her. "We must be patient. The captain promised to be here. He must have been delayed."

All the Jewish families stood around, surrounded by their trunks and household possessions, staring out beyond the port into the open sea, expecting to see ships appearing on the horizon at any moment.

Soon they heard instructions being shouted at them.

"All Jewish families awaiting the arrival of ships, step to the left. Come to the left loading dock immediately!"

The 20,000 picked up their children and possessions and crowded in front of the large loading dock to the left of the pier. Ten padres appeared on the dock carrying basins of baptismal water.

"There will be no ships today." One of the priests announced. "As we sprinkle this holy water on you, in the name of the Father, the Son and the Holy Spirit, you will become Catholic subjects of King Manuel of Portugal."

The priests waved their arms in wide arcs sprinkling water over the heads of those standing on the pier below.

Men, women and children started running backwards to escape the spray of the holy water. Many fell down in their eagerness to get away from the spray, and others fell over those on the ground. Children were crying.

Juanita clutched Luisa's skirt. "Mama, Papa what's happening? Why is everyone running and falling down? Is it raining? Where is our boat?"

Tomás bent over and picked up Juanita. "Hush, baby. We're going home now. Another day we will come back and ride on a boat."

The crowd of people on the pier shouted at the priests as they ran to escape the falling droplets. "Stop! You can't do this. We will not be Catholics! King Manuel gave us permission to leave Portugal."

Tomás and many of the men protested strongly to the king's soldiers at having been fooled into this conversion against their will, but there was nothing they could do. No one left the port that day by ship.

Tomás, Luisa, Juanita and Tomás' parents found a place to stay with friends in Lisbon.

"We should have known that it was only a trick when King Manuel insisted that everyone had to go to Lisbon on a certain day," Tomás told his father. They sat up late into the night with the other men of the house in which they were staying.

Luisa was feeding Juanita in the kitchen and was listening to the men talking through the open door.

"His advisors told him that it would be foolish to let all the Jews leave. He needed their counsel and also their taxes." Luisa heard one of the men say. "He decided to satisfy Queen Isabel's demands by converting us all, then there would be no Jews left in Portugal."

"My uncle is the king's war advisor," one of the men boasted. "He told me that King Manuel does not want to make all the Jews angry. He will not command his soldiers to spy on all our activities as Queen Isabel did. Maybe he'll let us live in peace."

The Martinez's had sold their home in Dagos. They found a new house right in Lisbon where many other Jewish families also lived. In fact there was a rabbi and synagogue there. They never saw royal soldiers on the streets.

Luisa and Tomás' son Fernando was born in Lisbon and two years later they were blessed with another son, Jose.

After a year of living in this Jewish section, Luisa became brave enough to take the silver candlesticks out of her trunk. Her neighbors taught her the Sabbath blessing that she had forgotten. She said it every Friday night as she lit the candles, surrounded by her family. She also placed her hands on the heads of each of her children and blessed them one at a time. Luisa was happy to be able teach her children some of the rituals of the religion she loved, but as she did, she always felt a little afraid. She always returned the candlesticks to the safety of the trunk when the Sabbath was over.

"Tomás, it is time that the boys start to go to the synagogue on the Sabbath. Will you take them?" she asked her husband one Saturday morning.

"Yes, of course," he answered. "It is time for me to learn something about my religion also. I will learn with them."

Luisa ran to give him a big hug. "Tomás, you have made me very happy! My parents were wise to choose you to be my husband!"

The years went by. Tomás took his sons to the synagogue every Saturday morning. The boys and their father took lessons in Hebrew. Luisa hoped that they would be able to become

B'nai Mitzvah when they reached thirteen. When Fernando turned 13 he became a Bar Mitzvah. To Luisa's surprise, Tomás had also learned to read the Torah portion from the holy scrolls and became a Bar Mitzvah also. After the ceremony, Luisa gave each of them a silver wine goblet with their names and the date engraved on them.

"Why can't I learn Hebrew with my brothers?" Juanita wanted to know. "After all, I am older than they are."

"I will teach you what Jewish girls need to know," Luisa told her. She taught her the Sabbath blessings. "When you are twelve, Juanita, I will give these silver candlesticks to you and you will take them to your home when you marry. It will be your responsibility to thank God for your home and family every Sabbath as my mother and grandmother did and as you see me doing now."

One Saturday around noon, Fernando and Jose came running into the house out of breath. "Mama, they took Papa. They are questioning him. The police have him at the police station."

"I must go there at once." Luisa started to get her cloak. "Quick, tell me what happened."

Fernando began, "We were walking home from the synagogue when some men yelled at our friends, who were walking right in front of us. Then some boys threw stones at us. They started to run away, but Papa ran after them. He caught one and was asking him why he threw the stones when a policeman appeared and grabbed Papa and took him away."

"It's starting again. I knew the peace wouldn't last. Juanita, watch your brothers. I'll be back soon."

Just then the door opened and Tomás walked in. "Papa, Papa!" the children ran to hug him.

Luisa just stared at him. "It's starting again, isn't it? Tomás what are we to do now?"

"Yes, Luisa, it's starting. Two men were killed last night as they were hurrying home before sundown. The police gave me a warning and told me to stay away from the synagogue."

"What does that mean Tomás?"

"It is not safe here in Portugal for Jews anymore. I have heard grumbles from some of my customers in the last few weeks. One told me that the padres are saying that Jews are disrespecting the Catholic religion even though they have all been made to convert. They have heard that some padres are organizing gangs of citizens to harass and murder Jews on the street and in their synagogues. I was hoping this was just a rumor, but today I learned that it is indeed true."

Again Jews appealed to King Manuel. They were afraid to stay in Portugal. They begged King Manuel to let them leave. He finally gave in.

Tomás' parents went to Turkey, but Luisa asked Tomás if they could go across the Ocean Sea so they could look for Felipe. They heard of a ship that would take them to Mexico.

⁘ ⁘ ⁘

Luisa was 30; Tomás was 47; Juanita was 15; Fernando was 13; and Jose was 9 when the Martinez family arrived in Taxco, Mexico on September 1, 1506. Capitan Colon died that same year and Luisa gave birth to her fourth child, her third son, the first of her children to be born in the new world. Tomás and Luisa named him Manuel.

"Mama, where is my uncle Felipe?" asked Juanita as they got off the ship. "You said we were crossing the ocean sea to be with your brother, my uncle Felipe. Is he here?"

"No Juanitacita. He is not here in Mexico, but he is not far away. He is on the island of Haiti. Your father will stay at this port city of Veracruz to inquire about ships leaving for Haiti. He will send a note to Felipe with one of the sailors going to Haiti. When Felipe gets the note I'm sure he will take the first ship he can to Veracruz. Then I can see my brother again and you and the boys will meet your Tio Felipe."

CLARA'S STORY

Taxco, Mexico, Fall, 1713

7

Jorge Seeks Adventure

"Tio Felipe swam to the island of Haiti when his ship was wrecked!" Jorge said over his shoulder to his brother, Pedro, as they ran toward the Mahogany tree.

"No, he landed on the coast of Mexico. That's why we live in Mexico now!" Pedro was running hard to keep up with his brother. "Ask Mama!" Their mother was sitting on a serape in the shade of the tree, rolling out tortillas on the flat stone she had scrubbed and now used especially for that purpose. Twelve-year old Clara was sitting there, too, braiding her long, black hair. Clara looked up as her younger brothers approached. Now what are they arguing about, she thought?

"Mamacita, where did Tio Felipe swim to when the Santa Maria was wrecked?" Jorge asked as he flopped down on the serape.

"His ship was wrecked on rocks, during a terrible storm, near the island of Haiti," Mother answered. "He and other sailors had to swim many miles to reach the island. There, brown skinned men with sharp daggers were waiting for them."

"Did Uncle Felipe have to fight the brown skinned men?"

"No, Jorge. When they saw that Felipe and the other sailors had no weapons the brown skinned men took them to their tents and fed them. They became friends."

"But Tio Felipe lived in Mexico." Pedro said. "When did he come here to Taxco?"

"It was many years later, Niño. He came to be with his sister, Luisa. She lived here in Taxco with her husband Tomás and their four children. Tio Felipe had not seen his sister since she was a young girl in Spain. She was twelve years old, I think. Sit down here in the shade, Niños. It's too hot to run around today. I'll tell you more stories about Tio Felipe."

The boys sat down. They liked to hear stories about their famous relative so they could brag to their friends about him and how he had braved the dangerous ocean sea with the great Cristobal Colon. Their friends may have had brave conquistadors, daring varqueros (cowboys) or saintly missionaries in their families, but no one had an ancestor like Felipe, who had sailed across the ocean with Capitan Cristobal Colon!

Mother told the stories that had been told to her when she had been a little girl.

"Felipe was only a year or two older than Clara, when he sailed away from Spain with Capitan Colon," Mother told them. "His parents didn't know his plans until it was too late to stop him. He was already on the ship!"

"Why would they want to stop him?" Jorge asked. "It would be an honor to travel with Capitan Colon!"

"Ocean voyages can be very dangerous, Jorge," Mother answered. "A ship could sink in a bad storm at sea. As you know, that's just what happened to the Santa Maria."

"But Felipe could swim." said Jorge.

"Yes, Jorge, Felipe was lucky. He was a strong swimmer and not too far from safety. But there were other dangers also. No one knew what Colon would find on the other side of the ocean sea. Some people even warned that his ships would drop off the edge of the earth."

"Now we know that couldn't happen," Pedro added. "The earth is round. Colon's trip proved that."

"That's right, Pedro. We don't have to be afraid of falling off the edge of the earth, but Felipe's mother also worried that she would never see her son again. As it turned out she was right about that."

"But my teacher told me that Capitan Colon sailed back to Spain. Why didn't Felipe go back with him?" Clara asked.

"Don't you remember, Clara, only two ships went back since the Santa Maria was wrecked." Jorge explained. "The crew from three ships would be too heavy for two."

"That may be one reason, Jorge. There were others also." Mother said.

"Maybe Felipe liked it better on this side of the ocean sea," Pedro suggested. "Maybe he didn't want to go home."

"There were many reasons some of the sailors did not go back to Spain, niños. You'll learn about them when you are a little older." Mother stood up, shaking bits of dough from her apron. "But now I must go into the house with these tortillas and help Maria prepare our noonday meal. Your father will be hungry and tired after riding home from the silver mines in this heat. Stay under the tree and play quietly until he arrives. Then we will all eat. After that - siesta!"

"Why is Papa coming home today, Mama? It is only Wednesday. Who will tell the workers what to do the rest of the week?" Clara asked.

"Papa has put one of the workers in charge. He will stay home with us this week until Monday. It is a special time for our family." She leaned over and whispered to Clara,

"You'll hear all about it tomorrow." Then she hurried into the house.

Special time? Clara wondered what her mother meant. What will I hear tomorrow? She started to follow her mother into the house, but her thoughts were interrupted by Jorge.

"If I had a chance to take an ocean voyage to explore new places, I would sneak away just like Felipe," said Jorge as he swung one leg over a low branch of the tree. "I know every corner of Taxco. I would like to see other places in the world, too."

Clara looked up at him swinging from the branch. "Don't talk like that, Jorge. You're much too little to go off by yourself. Don't you want to live where you have friends, cousins, uncles and aunts?"

"I would be afraid to leave my home," said Pedro. "And I would miss Bianca too much if I went away. I know she would be lonely for me, too. Who would feed her?"

"What a pequito niño you are, Pedro! Mama would feed your silly cat. I see Papa coming!" Jorge jumped down from the tree and ran toward his father.

Clara and Pedro ran to him, too. They reached their father as he was dismounting his horse.

"Papa, Jorge wants to run away like Felipe," Pedro told his father as he took his hand.

"What's this, Jorge? You want to run away?" Papa handed the horse's reins to him. "Here, first give Tompedo some water and oats and tie him under the Walnut tree. But I think it's too hot to run away today, don't you!"

"Oh, Papa, I didn't mean today. But I do want to see more of the world than Taxco and the silver mines." Jorge led the horse away.

Clara took her father's other hand. "Tio Felipe was very brave, wasn't he, Papa?"

"Yes, he was, Clara. Our family is very proud of him."

After washing their hands at the well, the three entered the house. Father took off his sombrero, flipped it with a circular motion across the entrance way where it landed squarely on the hat post there. Then he brushed his hand over the ceramic Madonna standing near the door and brought his fingers up to his lips in one quick motion.

Clara kissed the Madonna's cool cheek. Soon Jorge entered the house and everyone sat down to a midday meal of tortillas con carne, beans, tomatoes and mangos.

As Clara lay on her cot during the afternoon siesta, her thoughts turned again to Felipe. How would she feel if Jorge really did leave home to look for adventure? Felipe's sister Luisa traveled across the ocean just to find her brother. She must have missed him very much. Would I have been brave enough to do that, Clara wondered?

It was hard for Clara to imagine her own life anywhere but in Taxco, with her two brothers and her mother and father. She would even miss her two big cousins Diego and Carlos, even though they teased her endlessly, and their little sisters, Marina and Flora. No, she would never leave Taxco. She was happy and content here. This is where she belonged.

Then she remembered that her mother had said that the next day was a special one for their family. I love special days, she thought. She tried to imagine what would make it special.

8

The Special Day

It was Thursday. Mother and Father had greeted her cousins and uncle and aunt with warm hugs as they entered the house. But soon Mother shooed Jorge and Pedro, Marina and Flora out to play in the yard.

Clara kissed her beloved Madonna statue on her way to the big table in the eating room where she had been summoned by Uncle Antonio to join the grownups.

"You won't do that anymore after today," her cousin Diego said as he pulled out the heavy wooden chair at the table for her.

"Why not? I always kiss the Madonna as I walk past her," Clara told her cousin as she sat down. "So do Mamacita and Papa."

"They touch her feet and then kiss their fingers," said Diego, sitting down next to Clara, "that's different. After today you can ask them about it."

"QUIET!" boomed Uncle Antonio. The low buzz of conversation in the room stopped. "Take your seats. It's time to begin."

Clara's parents, uncle, aunt and older cousins sat down around the table. Mama had asked Clara to set the table that morning with her best embroidered cloth and the silver plates, platters and goblets. Clara thought that the table looked extra beautiful on this special day. She smiled as she looked around the table at her relatives. Suddenly she realized that something was missing.

"Where's the food?" Clara leaned over and whispered to Diego. The beautiful platters were still empty.

"Hush, Clara," said her mother. She gently put her hand in front of Clara's mouth as she sat down next to her.

By then Cousin Diego also had a hand over his mouth, his own, barely disguising the smirk he was sharing with his brother, Carlos, who sat at his other side.

But Uncle Antonio wasn't laughing and neither was her father. The two men sat across the table from Clara and her cousins. They both had looked up from their prayer books as they heard her whisper to Diego. Father glared at her and put his finger across his mouth.

Suddenly Uncle Antonio stood up and said, "Micaela, you didn't prepare Clara for this..."

"No, Antonio. You are head of the family, I thought, you would like, as usual, to make the first explanations to the children who have just joined our table." She stood up. "Tomorrow I will start to teach Clara the other things she needs to know."

When Antonio spoke again he no longer sounded angry. He spoke in a soft voice, almost a whisper. "Congratulations, Clara, on reaching your twelfth birthday."

"Thank you, Tio." Clara took her cue from her uncle and answered softly.

Antonio spoke to Clara again. "Now that you have celebrated your twelfth birthday I am going to tell you some things that you must never mention to anyone outside of this family. Can I trust you to secrecy?"

"Yes, Tio." She had always been a little afraid of her uncle, not only was his voice usually loud and sometimes quite gruff, but also he looked like a giant to her. She would never do anything to displease him.

"Good, then listen carefully. What you are about to hear is very important."

"Yes, Tio." Clara shifted forward in her chair and looked directly into her uncle's eyes.

"Clara, you see our whole family sitting around the table today as we do on many occasions. We like to gather the family together to celebrate happy days and to grieve sad ones. Usually the table is covered with platters of good food and Maria is bustling in and out of the kitchen. You have noticed that today is different. Is that so?"

"Yes, Tio."

Antonio looked at Clara's father. "Federico, why don't you continue."

Her father reached for Clara's hand across the table and gave it a squeeze. He looked into her eyes, let go of her hand, then began to speak. "Clara, every Sunday, since you were a little girl, your mother and I have taken you and your little brothers to Santa Javier Church to hear Mass. Isn't that right?"

"Yes, Papa." She frowned. What did Mass on Sunday have to do with no food today?

"Now that you are twelve it is time for you to know that although we go to Mass every Sunday, we do not attend because it is our religion. The religion of this family follows the laws of Moses, not those of the Catholic Church."

What? Clara couldn't believe what she thought she had heard. She looked around the table for confirmation of this strange information. She saw only serious expressions as she scanned the faces. She turned to her right. Diego looked at her as if to say, "Didn't I warn you?" She turned to her left. Her mother nodded.

Clara's stomach began to hurt. She knew it wasn't only because she was hungry. Her stomach always hurt when she worried about things.

The happy voices of her brothers and little cousins running and playing outside in front of her house drifted in through the open window behind her father. I wish I was out there with them, Clara thought.

Her father squeezed her hand again. "We only pretend to believe what is taught at Santa Javier every Sunday. In our hearts we follow the laws of Moses that our fathers, grandfathers and great grandfathers have passed down to us."

Clara stared at Uncle Antonio. Her mind was spinning. What was father telling her? Padre Juan had told of Jews who believed in the laws of Moses. What did her family have to do with the Jews? She tried to form an intelligent question that would not be disrespectful of her father, but before she could think of one her uncle continued.

"According to the laws of Moses, today is a fast day," he said. "It is a very holy day for us and for Jews all over the world. We will eat nothing this day until the sun goes down."

"But why are we sitting at the table if we are not going to eat?" She blurted out. "And why do we listen to Padre Juan every Sunday if we don't believe what he teaches?"

"Those are both very good questions, Clara," Uncle Antonio responded. "I'll try to answer them." He cleared his throat. "You have been taught that Mexico is part of Spain, is that right?"

"Yes, Tio."

"The Spanish king believes that everyone who lives under his rule must be a good Catholic. If he hears of Catholic men or women who do not follow all the beliefs of the Holy Church, in Spain or in Mexico, he orders terrible things to happen to them."

"What types of things happen to them?"

"Things that are too terrible for me to talk about now, Clara. Bad things could happen to all of us if you tell anyone, even your best friend, that our family is Jewish and follows the laws of Moses in our homes.

You asked why we are sitting at the table, but not eating. We do this so no one will become suspicious of us. If our neighbors, or even Maria, knew we were fasting on this Jewish holy day, they would have to tell the padre, and our lives would be in grave danger. The laws of Moses tell us to come together to fast and to pray on this day every year, but if the neighbors look in the window or come to the door they will see us at the table at lunch time with plates and platters in front of us. They will have nothing to report to the padre. Do you understand, Clara?"

"I think so, Tio. But I am VERY hungry."

Diego giggled.

"We are all hungry, Clara." Mother took her hand. "But now you must listen carefully again to Tio Antonio and I hope what you hear will help you to forget your hunger. I will answer the rest of your questions when we have some quiet time alone together. I will also teach you some prayers. But now it is time for Tio Antonio to lead us all in an afternoon of prayer."

✳ ✳ ✳

Clara could see the sun start to slip behind the mountains surrounding her little town, through the window behind her father's head. The last low rays caused long shadows to fall across the table. Her eyelids felt heavy, but she forced her eyes to stay open, if only to keep Diego from having something more to laugh at.

Uncle Antonio and the others were saying prayers to remember the family ancestors who had died. Of course Felipe was mentioned first, then his sister Luisa and her husband, Tomás and those who came after them.

Now as Clara sat with her head bowed, she was surprised to hear that her courageous ancestors Luisa, Tomás and Felipe had been Jews. They were being blessed for having had the courage to leave Spain and Portugal so they would be free to follow the laws of Moses and live as Jews openly and without fear.

That was the real reason they had crossed the ocean, she now knew, not just for adventure as she and all the children in the family had been told. Could she still brag about her brave ancestors?

Clara peeked up at Uncle Antonio. His head was still bowed. "Today we must pray together in secret in our homes," he continued, "but we hope that the day will come once more when we will have the freedom to pray openly to our God as did Luisa, Tomás and Felipe when they first arrived in the new world. Shema Yisrael, Adonai Echod. Hear O Israel, the Lord is One. Amen."

Chairs scraped on the tile floor. Clara opened her eyes and saw that everyone was getting up. Would they eat now?

Papa went quickly to light the oil lamps. Clara's mother and her aunt hurried into the kitchen. Clara went outside to stretch her legs and breathe some fresh air with the older cousins.

Diego was running to the end of the road. She held up her long skirt and tried to catch him. He had joined the table just last year. Maybe he would tell her how he had felt about it. But by the time she caught up to him, he was back in front of the house calling the little ones to come inside.

When Clara re-entered the dining room she saw that the once empty platters were now piled high with fish, bread and honey and hard-boiled eggs. Pitchers of wine and grape juice were on the table also.

The little children joined everyone at the table as the grownups ended their fast.

Food has never tasted this good, Clara thought.

When she had finished eating, Clara joined the card game her older cousins were playing. The cousins were laughing and noisy as they dealt out the cards. No one talked about the fast day or the prayers. How had they felt when they first found out the famous ancestors were Jewish? How could they play cards and laugh, as if there were no danger? Diego seemed totally engrossed in the card game. She couldn't ask him now.

"Clara, wake up! It's your turn to pick from the pile," cousin Carlos poked her in the side with his finger.

"Sorry." Clara picked a card and placed it in her hand. She tried to concentrate on the game, but soon she quit. Her head was muddled with questions about the day's revelations.

She sat down on the floor with the younger cousins. They were rolling a ball around in a circle. Clara kept missing the ball when it came to her.

"Clara, pay attention!" her brother Jorge shouted at her. I can't, thought Clara, and got up and left the circle.

She walked over to a chair in the corner of the front room, by the fireplace. Maybe if I just sit here and think, I'll be able to make sense of all I learned today, she thought.

She recalled a day last year or maybe the year before. She had fallen while playing outside with her cousins and came running in to show her mother her scraped knee. The relatives were sitting around the table, but no one spoke to her. She had wondered then why Mother had rushed her out of the house to clean her knee by the well and wrap a clean cloth around it.

Mother's words had seemed so odd to her that Clara still remembered them. "Don't run around for awhile, Clara, but stay outside! Don't come in again until I call you!"

Clara had had the feeling then, that something was happening in the house that she was not supposed to know about. But by the next day she had forgotten all about it. It must have been a fast day, she now realized.

Clara had heard about Jews in Sunday School. Padre Juan had said that they would not go to heaven, but she didn't know any Jews so she hadn't thought about it much. Now she HAD to think about it. If her whole family was Jewish, she was too. Her friends would hate her if they knew. What friends? She wouldn't have any friends.

I DO want to go to heaven, she thought. How will I be able to take Communion this Sunday, knowing that I am just pretending? Will Padre Juan think that I look different from last week? Will he be able to tell that I am Jewish? Is it because I am Jewish that it's been so hard for me to make my confessions to him? What will he do to me if he finds out?

After the relatives left, the house was quiet again. Clara's parents said nothing to her about the days events. Father was playing with her little brothers. Mother was busy in the kitchen.

Clara was exhausted. She kissed her parents and her brothers, but that night she did not kiss the Madonna. She went to her room, undressed, and got into bed. She twisted and turned, but she could not sleep. She was confused...she was also afraid. What terrible things might happen to her family, or even to her, if she forgot and told the secrets? Would they be killed? She didn't want to think about it, but couldn't stop.

Then another thought came to her. Just because my ancestors chose to follow the laws of Moses, maybe I don't have to. I choose to be a good Catholic!

Clara snuggled under her quilt. I'll tell Mamacita tomorrow. I really should have kissed the Madonna tonight.

9

The Decision is Too Difficult

"I've decided NOT to be Jewish," Clara blurted out cheerfully the next afternoon in her mother's bedroom. "I like being Catholic."

Mother stopped polishing the candlesticks she had removed from her trunk moments before. Her knuckles paled as she tightened her grip on them. She sat very still for a minute then looked up at Clara and resumed polishing.

"Clara, our family has always been Jewish. Many generations of our ancestors have worshiped God according to the laws of Moses here in Mexico and in Portugal and Spain before that.

She held the candlesticks up to the sunlight. Golden rays bounced off the shiny silver, streaking the walls and ceiling with light.

"In fact," Mother continued, "Luisa's parents even gave up their lives to remain faithful to the laws of Moses."

"That's very sad," Clara said. Then she stood up. Her shadow fell across the candlesticks, muting the bright glow in the room. "I'm afraid of dying, Mamacita, but when I do die, I want to go to heaven. Padre Juan said that Jews don't go to heaven. They burn in Hell!"

Mother set the candlesticks and cloth down on a little table. She took Clara's hand in hers.

"Remember what you heard yesterday. We don't believe all the things that Padre Juan teaches. Jews are good people and they do go to heaven!"

"Then why does Padre Juan tell us that they are evil?"

"Padre Juan must teach the beliefs of his Church, the belief that Jesus Christ is the son of God and only His followers will go to heaven. But the laws of Moses are older than those of the Catholic Church. Jews have been following them for four thousand years and don't want to be forced to accept Jesus Christ as the son of God."

"But I love Jesus and I love his mother, Mary. I kiss her statue by our front door everyday. I've seen you and father kiss her, too."

"You're right Clara, we do kiss her. I'll explain why we do soon, but first I want to tell you about the most important of the laws of Moses. It comes from the first of the ten commandments. Do you know it?"

"Yes. 'I am the Lord Your God' and 'You shall have no other Gods before me.'

"Good. Padre Juan taught you well. Jews believe that this commandment means that there is only one God, no son of God, no Holy Spirit, only one God. Whenever we pray we remind ourselves of this by saying four words: 'Sh'ma Yisroel Adonai Echod' which means, 'Hear O Israel, The Lord is One.' I'd like you to learn those four Hebrew words."

"If I say them will I be Jewish?"

"No, Clara. You will be Jewish only when you believe the words. I will teach you what I know and accept. I hope that someday you will believe as I do, and as your father believes, and as our ancestors before us believed. But we will not force you."

Mother let go of Clara's hand and walked toward the window. Without turning to face her she said, "As a good Catholic, you will be expected to give Padre Juan the names of the members of our family who follow the laws of Moses in secret."

Clara jumped up. "Mamacita," she said, running up to her mother at the window, "I would never do that! I would never put your lives in danger. What if you were killed because of me?"

Mother turned from the window. "That could happen," she said softly.

"Write down those four words for me. I will learn them."

"No. Someone might find the scrap of paper on which I wrote the words. You must listen carefully and repeat the words after me and remember them. Practice saying them to yourself when you are alone in your room, but always speak very softly. The servants must not hear them. Even your little brothers must not hear them. They are still too young to be trusted with this secret."

Mother took Clara's hand again as they sat down. They practiced the four words for a few minutes. "Sh'ma Yisroel Adonai Echod."

Then Mother stood up. "Enough for today, Clara. I'll listen to you again tomorrow. Now I must see where Pedro and Jorge are. It's too quiet in the house. Come back here when you see the sun begin its journey behind the mountains. Since it is Friday, I will tell you then about the most important Jewish ritual."

"Will I have to learn more Hebrew words?" Clara asked.

"Only a few more." Mother wrapped the candlesticks into the soft cloth, put them back into the trunk and closed its lid.

CRASH! Clara and her mother ran out of the door and peered over the balcony to the front hall below. The Madonna statue was lying on the tile floor in hundreds of pieces. In the middle of the clay shards lay a small leather ball.

"Caramba!" Mother said. "I knew I shouldn't take my eyes off of those boys for so long. Where are they? Pedro, Jorge get in here immediately!"

"Oh, no! My Madonna. All in pieces." Clara started to cry as she ran down the steps after Mother. "Why didn't I kiss her last night? It's my fault this happened!"

10

The Padre is at the Door!

"It's all my fault that our beautiful Madonna is broken!" Clara repeated as she searched for a piece of the Madonna's cheek. "I didn't kiss Her last night before I went to bed."

"Don't be silly, Clara," said Mother, turning over some of the larger pieces. "I've told your brothers a million times not to throw the ball in the house."

"Can we buy another Madonna?" Clara asked her mother.

"Of course we can, Clara, but it will be hard to find a special one like this one."

Mother knelt among the shards, picking up the larger ones. Suddenly she stopped. Under the ceramic piece that she held in her hand lay what looked to Clara like a little silver box. In one quick movement Mother scooped it up and put it down the front of her dress. Then she called the servants to sweep up the rest of the pieces.

"I'm going outside to look for the boys now, Clara." She tucked the leather ball under her arm, then started out the front door. Halfway out she paused, turned and said in a lower voice, "Don't forget to come back to my room when you see the sun going down."

Clara nodded distractedly. She caressed the ceramic cheek of the Madonna, which she had just picked up. When her mother had gone out the door she touched the shard to her lips, then took it to her room and put it under her pillow.

✼ ✼ ✼

The sun was slipping behind the mountains through the open window as Clara walked into her mother's room.

"Just in time, Clara." Mother looked up at her with a smile then she locked the door. "Please close the shutters."

"But it's so hot in here," said Clara reluctantly walking to the window.

"I know," Mother said, "We'll open them again soon. But for now they must be tightly shut."

Mother's double closet doors were open. The trunk had been pushed to the back again.

"I think I know the four words. Shall I say them to you?" Clara asked her mother.

"In a few minutes. We must do something else first. Watch and listen carefully as I welcome the Sabbath."

Mother glanced up at the shutters, then stood in front of two oil lamps that were on a shelf in the closet. She put a mantilla over her head, struck a match and lit the lamps. Clara watched intently as her mother moved her arms in a wave-like motion.

Mother covered her eyes with her hands and said, "Adonai, shel Shabat" three times. Then she opened her eyes and closed the closet doors, leaving the lighted oil lamps inside.

"You can open the shutters now Clara."

"Why did you close them?"

"Tio Antonio told me that Padre Juan climbs to the top of the church steeple and looks out over the houses surrounding Santa Javier on Fridays right after sunset to see if anyone has lit candles. The padre knows that lighting the candles on Sabbath Eve is very important to Jews since the Sabbath is the holiest of days. So....we light them in the closet. He can't see through closed doors!"

Clara walked slowly back from the window to where her mother was sitting at her dressing table, removing her mantilla. She sat down on her mother's bed. "Aren't you always afraid because of all the secrets you are keeping?" she asked.

"Yes, I am afraid a lot of the time, but I won't let that stop me from following the religion of my ancestors. They risked their lives to keep their beliefs. I don't want those risks to have been for nothing. I give meaning to their lives and my own by continuing the rituals as best I can. I hope you will feel the same way. When a Jewish girl becomes a wife and mother it becomes her duty to keep religion alive in her home."

"I'm not very brave." Clara looked down.

Mother reached over and lifted Clara's chin. "Neither was Luisa. She didn't want her parents to take chances by doing secret things. She left the silver candlesticks deep in her trunk for many years. Only when it was permitted to observe the Sabbath openly in Portugal did she take them out and light the candles. Then, when the danger to Jews started again, she knew she had to leave Portugal. She could live with secrets no longer."

"Is that when she sailed across the ocean to Mexico?"

"Yes, Clara. When she and Tomas and their children arrived in Taxco there were only Indians here, no Catholic Church, no padres. They could worship however they wanted without fear."

"I wish it was still that way. I always liked secrets, but not this kind. They scare me."

"Luisa and Tomás were able to live the rest of their lives openly as Jews. But shortly after their deaths the Spanish kings started sending padres here to New Spain to build churches and make sure everyone followed Catholic doctrines."

"That's when the candlesticks went back into the trunk?" asked Clara.

"Yes. The silver candlesticks will be yours when you marry. You're the oldest girl in the family. I hope one day you will be able to display them in the middle of your dining room table and not have to keep them in a trunk like I do. I light the oil lamps in the closet because I think the danger of fire is less, but when I cover my eyes, I see the flames of candles in Luisa's beautiful candlesticks."

Quick footsteps pounded up the stairs; then there was a loud knocking at the bedroom door. "Mama, mama come quick," called Pedro. "Padre Juan is at the front door."

"He wants to talk to you!" added Jorge.

Mother's face turned white. She stood up, looked in the mirror and smoothed her hair, tucking a loose strand into the bun at the nape of her neck.

"What could he want?" she said.

Clara crossed herself quickly. Had she not closed the shutters tight enough? Could Padre Juan have seen some light that slipped out under the shutters? God saw everything. Could God have told Padre Juan about the candles?

She followed her mother out of the room, but not down the stairs. She could see the front door from the balcony. Her brothers walked down the steps behind their mother with uncharacteristic decorum.

As Mother approached the door the boys followed right behind her. How brave she is, thought Clara.

"Buenas tardes, Padre Juan, come in," said Mother. "I am happy to see you." She swept her arm in an arc, indicating the door to the large front room. "Come sit down where we can be comfortable."

"Buenas tardes, Dona Micaela, I will not sit down because I will not be here long. I only came to ask you some questions." The padre's thin, tanned face was unsmiling. One hand was stroking the cross that hung on a chain around his neck.

Oh, no! thought Clara. What questions?

"Of course, Padre. How can I help you?" asked Mother. The little boys were peering out at the padre from behind her long skirt.

"I had a visit this afternoon from your servant girl, Maria, Dona Micaela. Frankly, what she told me has me quite concerned."

"But why are you telling me about it? What do her affairs have to do with me?"

"What she told me has much to do with you. Perhaps the boys should not be here."

Mother turned around and shooed the boys away. "Go to your room, niños."

They scrambled up the steps. Clara remained at her balcony listening post where the padre could not see her.

"Is your husband Don Federico, home?" asked Padre Juan.

"Not yet, Padre. He is visiting our relative Antonio Lopez who had a fever this week. I think Don Federico will be home soon. Perhaps you would like to wait for him."

"I cannot wait. And what I have to ask concerns you."

Clara gripped the rail of the balcony.

"What is it, Padre?" asked Mother.

"Dona Micaela, Maria has made a very serious charge against you today."

"Whatever could her charge be?" asked Mother. "I have hardly seen Maria today.

Padre Juan took a deep breath, straightened his shoulders and pulled his body up to its full height. "Maria told me," he then said, "that you, Dona Micaela, smashed the beautiful Madonna statue that always graced this entranceway of your home." He pointed to where the statue once stood. "I see that the statue is not here."

"No Padre. Maria is wrong. It was not I who smashed the Madonna."

✖ ✖ ✖

"Buenas tardes, Padre," said Clara as Padre Juan rushed by her on his way to her brothers' room.

"Buenas tardes," he said quickly, not stopping.

He entered the boys' room without knocking and closed the door behind him. Clara looked over the balcony toward the front door again. Mother was sitting on a small bench. Her head was bowed. Was she praying?

In a few minutes the padre reappeared, descended the stairs quickly, tipped his hat to Clara's mother and was out the front door.

Clara went downstairs when the door had closed behind him. Mother put her arm around Clara's shoulder. "You're right, Clara. We must get a new Madonna right away."

Mother was holding, in her clenched fist, the little silver box she had picked up from the shards on the floor earlier that day. "But it will be difficult to find another one with a special place to hold this." She opened her hand and showed the silver box to Clara.

"What is it, Mamacita?"

"This box contains a parchment scroll with the "Sh'ma" prayer written on it in Hebrew letters. Jews put it near their front doors to keep their homes safe. We touch it whenever we pass it, even when it is hidden in a Madonna's foot."

Clara's mother kissed the box and put it back down the front of her dress. "It didn't take long for our good fortune to change when the scroll was not at the door!"

ANA'S STORY

Taxco, Mexico, Spring, 1835

11

Trouble On the Plaza

Ana took a deep breath as she stepped out of St. Loretta's Church. She gazed across the sun-streaked plaza. Small children were running around playing with hoops and balls. Couples were walking slowly, arm in arm, in the shade of the trees along the perimeter. Flowers were everywhere!

I could stand here forever, she thought. Everything smells so good!

But Holy Week was a busy time in her town of Taxco. She knew she was needed at home to help her great grandmother, Bonita, with the Easter baking. Suddenly she remembered how Noni, that was what she called her great grandmother Bonita, had looked that morning. She flew down the steps of the church.

Mother, Grandmother and her little sister Lucia were delivering Easter flowers to sick friends. Father, Grandfather and Pedro were setting up booths at the far end of the plaza.

Ever since Ana had been a very little girl she had helped with the Easter baking. But that morning, as Ana had kissed Noni's cheek, she thought that her great grandmother had looked especially tired. Ana had promised to hurry home.

"Noni Bonita, don't start baking until I get home," she had said. "I'll be back to help you right after Mass." But even as Ana spoke, her great grandmother was shuffling across the kitchen to the pantry where the heavy clay mixing bowls were stored.

Ana started to run across the plaza, but stopped suddenly. Who was shouting? She heard angry words. It sounded like, "Christ Killer" and "Jew."

She looked around.

Across the square boys were running around a bench on which a very old man was sitting. They were shouting at him. Ana had often seen him there before. Why were the boys shouting at him today?

Others were walking toward the bench. Ana followed them. As she neared it she saw that the boys were throwing things at the old man. She had never seen anyone do that before.

There was her friend, Benno! His hand was raised. His face was twisted and menacing. Was that a stone in his hand? She had to stop him!

"Benno, stop! Leave the old man alone!" Ana moved in front of her friend, waving her arms. "Why are you calling him names? He's an old man. Leave him alone!"

The old man held one hand over his eyes, shielding them from the debris. His other hand clutched a square, cracker-like piece of bread.

Some of the adults who had stopped near the bench joined in with the jeers, "Christ killer. Jew!" But most just stood silently and watched. Their silence seemed to give the boys encouragement.

"Get out of my way, Ana. This has nothing to do with you! Can't you see what the old man has in his hand?" Benno gruffly pushed her aside, threw the stone that was in his hand and scooped up some straw off the plaza ground. As he threw the straw he shouted, "This is what you get, Jew. Go ahead, eat that flat bread. Eat the bread of the Jews. Christ killer!"

Ana felt her face get hot as she heard her friend's shouts. Why did he call the flat bread, "bread of the Jews"? Her own great grandmother baked that bread every Easter! She wasn't a Jew! Didn't Jews have horns on their heads? Should she explain to Benno? No, not today.

Ana took another quick look at the man on the bench, then turned away from the crowd and started running toward her home. Tears were rolling down her cheeks. She'd ask Noni about the flat bread.

At home Ana stopped outside of the closed kitchen door. How should she ask

Noni Bonita? Should she tell her about the old man and the boys? Should she tell her that Benno called the flat bread the "bread of the Jews"? Maybe Noni knew that was what the bread was called.

Ana used the bottom of her flowered skirt to wipe away her tears. She smoothed down her long, black hair and straightened her blouse. She took a deep breath, slowly turned the knob, then pulled open the kitchen door and stepped inside.

Her great grandmother was leaning over the open clay oven, spatula in hand, turning two crispy squares of flat bread.

"Hello, Noni Bonita," Ana said, trying to sound normal. She gave her great grandmother a quick kiss on the cheek.

"I'm glad you're back, Ana," Noni responded. She put down the spatula, then turned from the hot oven. "Ana, your face is all red! What have you been doing? Do you feel all right?"

"I feel fine, Noni. I just ran all the way home so I could help you."

"Maybe you have a fever. Let me feel your forehead."

"I'm fine," Ana ducked away from Noni Bonita's extended hand. "What do you want me to do?"

"There's not much left to do, Ana, but I am tired. You can roll out the rest of the dough." Noni Bonita shuffled over to the kitchen table and sat down heavily in a chair beside it. "I didn't want to miss Holy Wednesday Mass, but there's so much Easter baking to be done, and I don't move as fast as I used to. Were the flowers beautiful in church today?"

Ana tucked a long towel into the ruffled top of her lace blouse and rinsed her hands in the bucket of water on the floor. "Yes, Noni, they were. I told Padre Alonzo that you were very tired this morning."

She took a handful of the stiff dough from the clay bowl on the table, rolled it out on a wooden board into a rectangle and cut the rectangle into two squares. She pricked the squares with a sharpened stick and put them in the oven, replacing the crisp ones that she had just removed and placed on a cooling rack.

Finally Ana sat down by her great grandmother, who patted her hand approvingly. She had been intently watching each step of Ana's preparation of the cracker-like bread.

"Noni Bonita," Ana said softly, "why do we bake this flat bread?"

"We bake it to keep the memory of my blessed mother alive. She always baked it at Easter time."

"But, Noni, why did your mother bake it?"

"Because her mother did. We always ate it with celery and a glass of wine. My grandmother called it 'mazza.'"

"Noni, a man was eating 'mazza' like this in the square today."

"In the plaza? You must be mistaken. My mother never let me take the flat bread out of the house." Noni Bonita gazed out of the window. "We only ate the 'mazza' in the casa. And when the padre came to our home we only offered him tortillas and peppers stuffed with eggplant. No meat during Holy Week and no mazza for the padre. My mother always said 'no mazza for the padre.'"

"Noni, do you know why your mother said that?"

Noni Bonita looked at Ana. "My mother warned me, 'If you take the mazza out of the casa or give it to the padre there might be trouble.' Why are you asking all of these questions, Ana?"

"Some boys were throwing stones at the man in the plaza, and they were yelling terrible things at him."

"What were they yelling, Ana?"

Ana told her what she had seen and heard that morning.

"Benno wasn't right, was he? Our flat bread isn't 'the bread of the Jews' is it?

Noni Bonita took Ana's hands in hers. She gazed deep into Ana's eyes. After a few moments she spoke. "Maybe it's time, Ana, for you to learn something about your ancestors."

12

A Fire!

For a few minutes Noni Bonita said nothing. Ana leaned back in her chair, waiting for her great grandmother to begin.

"When I was about your age, she said at last, my mother, Clara, explained to me that our ancestors ate the 'mazza' around Easter time because the laws of Moses commanded them to. Have you heard about the laws of Moses?"

"Yes, Noni. Padre Alonzo taught us that Jews follow the laws of Moses and they don't follow the teachings of Christ! Our ancestors weren't Jews, were they?"

Noni Bonita closed her eyes. Ana waited for her to answer, but Noni's eyes stayed closed. Ana leaned forward and gently shook her great grandmother's shoulder. "Noni, our ancestors weren't Jews were they?" she repeated.

It seemed to take a lot of effort, but finally Noni Bonita raised her heavy eyelids. She searched out Ana's eyes again. "Yes, Ana. Our ancestors were Jews."

"Oh, no!" Ana sucked in her breath. "What if Padre Alonzo finds out?" She stared back at Noni Bonita. "Are you a Jew? Is my mother a Jew? Am I a Jew, too? I don't want to be called a Christ killer. I love Jesus!"

She pulled her hands out of Noni's and backed away from her. "If I'm a Jew Padre Alonzo won't let me take communion. I'll burn in hell!" Ana's eyes filled with tears.

"Come back and sit down, Ana. You are not a Jew. You have been brought up a good Catholic. That is what you are."

Ana walked slowly back to her chair next to Noni Bonita. "Then why do WE eat mazza if it is something that Jews are supposed to eat? Why do WE have to eat it?"

"We don't HAVE to eat it. I told you why I bake it. It is only out of respect for my mother and those who came before her that I bake it."

"I don't think we should bake the mazza anymore," Ana mumbled.

"You go to Mass and confession with your family every week. You will not be called a Christ killer. Your mother and father, your grandmother and grandfather follow the teachings of the Church. That is good. Everyone respects our family in Taxco. I am the only one left in the family who remembers anything about the laws of Moses and I am telling you about them now only to explain to you what you saw in the plaza today."

Noni Bonita wiped the tears off of Ana's cheeks with the edge of her apron and took Ana's hands into hers again. "Listen carefully. When I married your great grandfather I pushed my ancestors' beliefs to the back of my head and decided to accept with my whole heart the beliefs of the Catholic Church. All my life I had heard stories of the persecution of my ancestors for being Jews. I decided the suffering of our family must end. I wanted my children and grandchildren and great grandchildren to be safe and live without fear."

"Does Mama know that our ancestors were Jews? Does Grandma know? Why didn't anyone tell me?"

"Yes, they know. Your mother was going to tell you all about our family on your twelfth birthday next month."

Ana looked at Noni with disbelief. She had always thought her family was very ordinary, just like every other family in Taxco. Did other families have secrets, too, or just hers?

Noni Bonita continued, "Ana, every oldest daughter in our family, when she reaches the age of twelve, is taught about our ancestor's traditions. When you marry your mother will give you the silver candlesticks that have been passed down to the oldest daughters in our family for many, many generations. We honor the memory of our ancestors in this way and pray, as they did, when we light the candles on Fridays at sunset, that the evil spirits will stay far away from our home."

"Noni, did our ancestors light candles because they were Jews?"

"Yes, Ana."

"Does Padre Alonzo know that we light special candles at home?"

"No, Ana. And you must not tell Pedro and Lucia about the candles either. They are too young to understand the need for secrecy. The townspeople may misunderstand why we light them and call us names like they called the old man. We know that the Jews did not kill Christ, but long ago people who hated Jews spread this story."

"Will you show the candlesticks to me? Can I see them now?"

"No. Your mother will show them to you. But remember this. We do not light the candles to disrespect the Catholic Church. We light them only to carry on a family tradition and to keep our family safe. You have my permission, as I gave it to your grandmother and mother, to forget all about the laws of Moses and follow the teachings of Jesus with all your heart. Padre Alonzo is a good man, I have known him for a long time." She kissed Ana's cheek.

※ ※ ※

"Oh what a smell." Grandmother and Mother came rushing into the kitchen, crossing themselves as they ran. "Mama you've burned the bread!" said Grandmother. Black smoke was curling out of the clay oven and filling the kitchen.

Ana ran to the oven, grabbed the spatula and shoved it under the now black squares of flat bread. They crumbled and fell to the floor. "I'm sorry. It's my fault. I'll clean it up." She grabbed the broom and started sweeping up the charred crumbs.

Noni Bonita shook her head. "Ana and I were talking. I guess I'm getting too forgetful to bake bread. What a mess we made in your nice clean kitchen, Mariana. I'm sorry."

"Noni, you better get some rest. You've been baking all morning, I'm sure you're tired." Mother turned to Ana, "Ana, you stay and help clean the kitchen. How much more flat bread do we have to bake? I have to start on the tortillas!"

"It looks like there is only enough dough for two more squares," Grandmother said, looking into the bowl. "I'll roll them out, then we can finish the Easter baking. Ana, open the shutters so we can get rid of this smoke. Your mother just finished scrubbing the walls and floors to get ready for Holy Week! Maybe the burning was a sign that it's time to stop baking the flat bread. There's so much else to do at Easter time!"

Noni Bonita sighed and lifted herself out of the chair. She leaned heavily on her cane as she walked out of the room. She was moving her head from side to side slowly. "That's never happened to me before," she said softly. "I'm always so careful not to burn the bread."

⁂

The smoke was out of the house and the last two crispy squares of flat bread had long been stacked on top of the previously cooled ones.

Mother and Grandmother had been busy baking tortillas, cooking fish and stuffing peppers most of the afternoon. Ana knew that after Holy Wednesday no more work could be done until the end of Easter. She had done what she could to help them. No one spoke of the burned flat bread anymore. Ana thought about all that Noni Bonita had told her, but decided that this was not a good time to ask her mother any questions.

In the late afternoon, along with the other women in the village, Mother and Grandmother went back to Santa Loretta's to pray the Thirty-three Credos.

Ana went to Noni Bonita's room. Her great grandmother was sitting at her drawing table with a large sheet of paper in front of her. "Noni, do you want me to help you walk to the garden so you can paint there?"

Noni Bonita's arm swung over the table to cover the paper in front of her and turned toward the door. "Oh, it's you Ana," she said. "No, I don't want to go to the garden, I'm busy here."

"What are you drawing? Is it for Easter?"

"No, it's not for Easter." She stared at Ana for a minute. Then she said slowly, "I wasn't going to show this to anyone. But maybe it's a good thing you are here. I'm going to need your help. It took me longer than I thought to finish."

Ana walked over to the table and gently removed her great grandmother's arm from the paper. "It's beautiful, Noni. So many flowers just like in church this morning. But it doesn't look complete. There are no flowers in the middle."

"It's finished, Ana. I will leave it the way it is." Noni Bonita rolled up the paper carefully. "Will you help me now?"

"Of course, Noni. What do you want me to do?"

"Have your mother and grandmother gone to Santa Loretta's?"

"Yes, Noni."

"Is your father home?"

"No, Noni. He and Grandpa are helping with the fiesta in the plaza. Lucia and Pedro are there, too."

"Good." Noni Bonita handed the roll to Ana. "I'd like you to take this to the stonecutter. He is expecting it. He knows just what to do with it. All you have to do is to tell him it is from me. Will you do it?"

"Of course, Noni. Shall I go right away?"

"Yes. You must go right away because he will be going to Santa Loretta's with all the men as soon as night falls. I want you to take it now while your mother and grandmother are at church. They must know nothing about it. Can you keep this secret?"

"I'll do whatever you ask, Noni."

13

Noni Bonita is Very Sick

"Did your mother show you the candles yet, Ana?"

"No, Noni." Ana put a cup of hot tea down on the table by her great grandmother's bed.

"What month is this?"

"It's May, Noni, May 5th. My birthday is in two weeks, May 19th." Ana straightened her great grandmother's blankets, then gave her a kiss on the cheek.

"I guess she's waiting until then. But I don't think I'm going to last that long."

"Oh, Noni. Don't say that!" Ana took Noni Bonita's hand. "I can't celebrate my birthday without you!"

"Sit down, Ana. There are some important things I want to talk to you about before I die." Noni Bonita held a handkerchief to her mouth as she coughed.

"Noni, don't talk like that. You're going to get well."

"Your mother should have reminded me that you are almost twelve. I have to tell you things, but this cough…" Noni turned her head away. Soon she turned back. "I'm getting very weak, Ana."

"Mama said I should make sure you drink all of the tea. It will make you feel better. Here, take some now." Ana held the cup up to Noni Bonita's lips. "Señora Torres brought over herbs from her garden for this tea. She told Mama that these herbs are special and will make you strong again."

Noni Bonita took a sip of the tea, then coughed into her handkerchief again. "Oooh, this tastes terrible. Maybe Señora Torres didn't like the soup I took to her husband last month."

"She told Mama that it will make your cough go away. Drink some more." Ana held the cup to Noni Bonita's lips again.

"I hope she's right." She took another small sip. "Now, Ana, listen carefully. I have to tell you some more things today that you can not talk about to anyone." Noni Bonita closed her eyes and tried to take a deep breath. She coughed again.

Ana gazed at her great grandmother. She loved her very much. Why was it so hard for Noni to breathe? What could she do to help her? Her eyes filled with tears. Her great grandmother looked very frail.

In a few moments Noni opened her eyes and started speaking again, "I told these things to your grandmother and to your mother when they were twelve." She paused again, but squeezed Ana's hand as she did.

Ana held the cup up again. "Take another sip first, Noni."

"No more, Ana, put the cup down and listen to me."

Ana put the cup on the night table.

"Ana, I notice that you keep your jump rope in the urn by the front door."

"That's right, Noni. But I'm always careful. I know you made that urn and I don't want to knock it over and break it."

"It's a good place for the jump rope. But I'm glad that you are careful when you are near it because it is not just a clay pot to put things in. It has magic powers, too!" Noni Bonita coughed again, then closed her eyes.

"What can it do, Noni? How can a clay pot be magical?"

Noni took a raspy, shallow breath and opened her eyes again.

"Listen and I will tell you. My grandmother, Micaela, asked me to make the urn for her when I was about your age. When the clay was still wet she asked me to scoop out a pocket near the bottom of the urn. Then she gave me a little silver box to place in the pocket. She told me to seal the pocket and smooth it over to look like the rest of the urn. After I had done all that, she told me that our family would always have good luck while the urn stood by the front door of our home."

"Is that the magic, Noni?"

"Yes, Ana." Noni Bonita's voice was only a whisper. "The box that is hidden in the urn has magical powers to keep the people in the house safe. My grandmother told me to touch the urn with my fingertips when I pass it, then kiss my fingers to show respect for the magic of the silver box. She also told me that the magic will only work if no one outside of the family knows that the box is there." Noni Bonita coughed again.

She put her handkerchief down, took Ana's hand and looked directly into her eyes. "You must not tell your friends about the silver box and its magic. You must not tell Lucia or Pedro either because they are still too young to be trusted with this secret."

"Do you know what's in the box, Noni? Is it magic dust or an amulet?"

"My grandmother told me that the box holds a tiny scroll with some writing on it. I'm sure she told me what it says, but I can't remember anymore. All I remember is that it must be kept secret to bring luck and it can bring trouble to the family if the neighbors find out about it." Noni closed her eyes.

"I'll keep the secret, Noni," Ana leaned closer and whispered. "Did our Jewish ancestors hide scrolls in urns, too?"

"I don't think so, Ana. But the scroll was important to my grandmother. I think it was given to her by her mother. It probably came from the Jewish ancestors. She asked me to hide it in the urn to keep *it* safe and to touch the urn when I passed it to keep *me* safe. Now I must sleep for a while. I'm very tired. Come back later."

Ana picked up the tea cup, kissed Noni Bonita's cheek, and left the room. The urn stood near the bottom of the stairs at the side of the front door. Ana put the cup down on the step and gently pushed the urn over on its side so she could inspect its base.

She ran her fingers over the smooth, cool clay. "I don't feel anything unusual," she mumbled as she rotated the base. Then she kissed her fingers just to make sure she hadn't broken any spells.

"What are you doing, Ana? Why did you knock the urn over?" It was her little brother, Pedro.

Ana jumped up. "Oh, where did you come from?" She stood the urn upright again. "Why don't you have your shoes on? I didn't hear you." She picked up the teacup.

"It's hot. Mama said I could play barefoot today." He sat on the bottom step and put his sandals on. "Papa is taking Lucia and me up to the silver mines in a little while. But what were you doing? I keep my ball in the urn. Don't break it!"

"I was just looking at the bottom of it. See, I didn't let your ball roll out."

Pedro had a quizzical look on his face. "What's on the bottom of it?"

"Nothing," said Ana.

"Then why were you looking at it?"

"No reason. I wondered why Noni strokes it all the time. But I couldn't find anything."

"Noni strokes it? I never saw Noni touch it."

"Well maybe you're right. I probably just dreamed that I saw Noni touch it.

"Is Noni going to die?" Pedro asked.

"Of course, someday she will. I hope not soon, but be very nice to her and play quietly because she's sleeping."

"I'll be quiet." Pedro went outside.

Ana went into the kitchen where her mother was standing in front of the stove and her grandmother was cutting vegetables at the kitchen table.

"How's Noni?" Ana's mother asked without turning around. "Did she drink the tea?"

"She drank most of it, but she's still coughing. Then she got tired and sent me away. She's sleeping now." Then in a lower voice Ana added, "Noni told me about the magic of the urn. Do you believe it?"

"Now it's magic is it?" Ana's grandmother stopped chopping. "When she told me about the urn many, many years ago she said the box hidden in it had something to do with Moses in the Bible. If someone accidentally knocked the urn over and broke it we would have a good excuse to inspect that little box."

Ana's mother crossed herself. "Mother, don't say that!" she said. "I wouldn't want anything to happen to it. It's always been so important to Noni. I don't care what's in the silver box. I will always treasure the urn that Noni made, and I even try to remember to touch it when I walk by. I don't take chances with bad luck either."

Ana didn't like to hear her mother and grandmother arguing. She walked over to the fireplace. "What are you cooking?" she asked. "It smells good."

"It's a chicken frittata, Ana. We made the fish stew for tonight this morning."

Grandmother scraped the vegetables she had been cutting into the pot and stirred them up with the chicken.

"It's because of Noni that we cook two meals every Friday, isn't it?" Ana asked.

"That's right," Mother answered her. "Noni said that her mother and grandmother always did that so they wouldn't have to cook on Saturday."

"And one dish had to be chicken and the other fish," added Grandmother.

"And," Mother continued, then both of them said in unison, "don't tell the neighbors."

"That's what she said about the urn, too," said Ana. "Why is everything so secret? I don't think the neighbors care what we do."

"I don't think they do either, Ana," said Grandmother. "Times are changing, but I think when Noni Bonita was young her mother taught her to be afraid of the neighbors. Maybe that's why she always takes them soup when they are sick. I'll go upstairs now and see if she needs anything."

"Ana, did Noni tell you about the old candlesticks that I light every Friday night?" asked Mother as she wiped off the kitchen table.

"Yes she did, but I never saw you do it."

"The family tradition is that the light from the candles in these candlesticks must be kept hidden. I have always been careful to go to the pantry and light them there when you and Pedro and Lucia were busy playing or not at home. But now you are almost twelve. It's time for you to know about them. The candlesticks have been in our family a long time. You're the oldest daughter; they will be yours when you marry."

"I know; Noni told me. Can I see them?"

"Let's light them in Noni's room tonight. It might cheer her up a little. The sun will be going down soon. Go up to her room and close the shutters tightly. I'll be up with the candlesticks and candles soon."

14

A Death

When Ana returned to Noni Bonita's room her great grandmother had turned her body toward the wall. Ana's grandmother had squeezed a chair between the bed and the wall and was sitting there holding her mother's hand.

"Noni is very weak, Ana. You better tell your mother to come up here quickly and then you can get the padre."

"No padre, no padre," Noni whispered. "Not yet, no padre."

"Mama is bringing up the candlesticks, Grandmother," Ana said. "Do you think Noni will like seeing them lit?"

"Yes, I think she will like that. You had better close the shutters," Grandmother said to Ana. Then she spoke to her mother again. "It's Friday night. We will light the candles here tonight. Will you like that?"

Noni Bonita nodded. "My mantilla," she whispered. Then she looked at Ana closing the shutters. "Watch what your mother does." She coughed again. "Light the candles every Friday. Don't tell the neighbors."

Grandmother draped a mantilla over Noni's head and put one over her own. She handed a small scarf to Ana. Then she went back to her chair next to the wall.

No one spoke. Only Bonita's shallow raspy breathing broke the silence.

✣ ✣ ✣

"They're beautiful, Mama." Ana stood up and went over to get a closer look at the candlesticks that her mother had just brought into the room. A few rays of golden sunlight that had squeezed under the closed shutters were reflected in the silver of the candlesticks. They seemed to glow. Ana rubbed her fingers over the filigreed silver. Then Mother put the candlesticks on the table by Noni Bonita's bed.

No one spoke. When the sunlight had faded, Noni watched intently as Mother lit the candles, circled the flames with her hands then covered her eyes. Noni, Mother and Grandmother whispered, "Adonai, Shema" in unison. Then Noni started to cough again. This time when the coughing subsidedd she pointed to her rosary beads. Grandmother handed them to her.

The room glowed with the candlelight. It was quiet except for the soft clicking of the rosary beads accompanied by Noni's soft, muffled sounds. "Shema" then silence, clicking of the beads, then "Adonai, Adonai" then a long silence and again, but much slower, the soft clicking of the beads.

Mother looked at Grandmother. "I think it's time," she said. "We must get the padre."

"No padre," Noni rasped very softly, "no padre."

"We must have a padre, Mother. You must confess your sins. You want to go to heaven." Grandmother spoke softly to Noni, then to Ana. "Run and get the padre, Ana. Run quickly."

Ana found Padre Alonzo reading by the light of an oil lamp on the porch of his house, next to the church.

"*Excuse*, Padre Alonzo, come quickly. My great grandmother Bonita is dying. *Por favor* come quickly." Then Ana ran back to her house and waited for the padre at the front door.

The candlesticks were no longer in Noni's room when Ana and Padre Alonzo entered. A single oil lamp on the table next to Noni Bonita's bed provided a dim light.

Grandmother got up from the chair between the bed and the wall and motioned for the padre to sit there. Noni hadn't moved. She was still facing the wall, slowly fingering her rosary and very softly mumbling two barely recognizable sounds over and over again with long gaps of noisy breathing in between, "Shema"..... "Adonai"........... "Shema"................ "Adonai".....then nothing.

"Can you take her confession, Padre?" Mother asked.

Padre Alonzo put his little leather sack holding the sacramental oil on the table. He then put on his purple stole for giving final unction and sat down next to Noni Bonita's bed. He leaned over her and tilted his head so his ear was next to her lips.

"Will you take her confession, Padre?" Mother asked again.

Padre continued to listen to Noni with his ear near her lips. He lifted his head and looked at Mother, then at Grandmother. "Bonita was a good woman," he said. "She sent her children to mass and confession each week. She always helped the needy and orphans in our parish. She helped me raise money to build a new bell tower after the fire." He took off his stole, folded it and laid it on the table next to the leather sack of oil. "Let her die in peace. Let her die in peace."

"But her confession, Padre, what about her last confession?" Grandmother asked.

He gazed into the eyes of Ana's mother and grandmother. They were standing at the foot of the bed with questioning looks on their faces. Then he looked into Ana's eyes. "Do not speak of this to anyone," he said to all three. His gaze lingered, for a second time, on each pair of eyes. "Let her die in peace," he repeated once more. Then he crossed himself, picked up his sack and stole and walked out of the room.

By the time the echo of his shoes on the steps had dimmed to silence, so had the sounds in Noni Bonita's room. No more raspy breathing, no more softly clicking rosary beads, no more whispered words were heard.

Grandmother put her hand over Bonita's mouth. She moaned softly, crossed herself and gently drew her mother's eyelids down over her eyes. Noni Bonita was gone.

Dear Bonnie,
  Thanks for your letter. I can't tell you anything about Luisa or Tomás, but I have seen the candlesticks. My grandmother Ana showed them to me a few years ago. They had been given to

her by her great grandmother Bonita. In fact, I wonder how your grandmother, Sofia, got them because Ana promised that she would leave them to me in her will. Ana was very old when she died, so she must have gotten mixed up. Instead, I got a silver wine goblet with the name Tomás and the date 1513 on it. Keep in touch, and let me know what you find out.

*Sincerely,
Rosita Rodriguez
220 Sixth Ave.
San Jose, California 95103*

EPILOGUE

San Francisco, California; The Present

I

Part One

"Do you think we'll recognize her?" Margarita asked her mother. They were standing in the San Francisco bus station waiting for the bus from Tucson to pull into its slot in the station's garage. "It shouldn't be too hard, I think," Margarita's mother answered, "Last time that I took a long bus trip most of the passengers were middle aged or older. Not too many young girls travel on the bus alone. She said she'd be wearing a yellow shirt didn't she?"

"Yes she did." said Margarita, "That should make it real easy." "Let's go stand right in front of the window, so we'll have a clear view of the passengers as they step off the bus."

"Here comes the bus!" Margarita sounded very excited.

"There she is! Do you see her, Mom? She looks just like Carmen. Let's wave, so she'll know we see her."

"All right! Good idea. Then she won't have to wander around the bus station looking for us. You're right she does look like your cousin, Carmen!"

The girl in the yellow shirt went up to Margarita and asked, "Hi! Are you Margarita? I'm Bonnie."

"Hi Bonnie. Yes, I'm Margarita. I'm so happy you could come!"

"Hello, Bonnie, I'm Margarita's mother. We are both very glad you could come to San Francisco to visit us. How was the bus ride?"

"I'm used to buses. I don't mind the ride as long as the bus isn't too packed so I can have the whole seat to myself. I did get the whole seat all the way from Tucson, so I could stretch out. I think I even slept a little after I ate my sandwich."

"That's good." They left the bus station and got into Margarita's family car. Margarita's mother drove out of the parking lot, then said, "We haven't planned anything special for this afternoon so you girls can get acquainted, Bonnie, but maybe you'd like to wash up first. Then we can have a little snack. How does iced tea and cookies sound to you, Bonnie?"

"Perfect! I am very thirsty and I always have room for cookies!"

"Then that's what we'll do." Margarita's mother pulled the car into the driveway of their home. They entered the house. "Margarita, take Bonnie and her bag up to your room. Then show her where the bathroom is. She'll probably feel like washing up. I'll put out the tea and cookies on the kitchen table. Bonnie, you'll meet Margarita's father and brothers at dinnertime. They are all at soccer practice this afternoon. There's a big game tomorrow. Margarita wants you to meet Aunt Laura. I'll drive you girls down to L.A in the morning.

We'll have to get a real early start so I can get back before the game is over. Bonnie, it's a long drive to L.A., I'm sorry that we won't have enough time to take you down along the scenic coastal route, but instead we'll take the inland route through Santa Barbara. That only takes about five hours."

"That's fine with me," said Bonnie," I've never seen any of California so everything we see will be interesting to me."

Margarita picked up Bonnie's suitcase and headed up the stairs, "Come on, Bonnie, follow me!"

"OK. Here I come. I can carry my suitcase by myself."

"No, that's all right. I've got it! You're the guest. The suitcase is very light. Did you remember to bring the silver candlesticks?"

"Yes, they're in there," said Bonnie.

"I'm really excited to see them. Do you think they're really 500 years old?"

"You can see for yourself. The date is right on them. But first, show me the bathroom. I would love to take a shower. I feel so grubby!"

Margarita took a towel from the hall closet. "Here is your towel, Bonnie. That second door on the right is the bathroom."

Bonnie took off her yellow shirt and jeans in Margarita's bedroom, then ran down the hall, holding the towel around her.

When Bonnie returned to Margarita's bedroom about ten minutes later, the towel was wrapped around her head. She had another towel wrapped around her body like a sarong. As Bonnie took a clean shirt and pair of jeans out of her suitcase she also took out two narrow packages, each wrapped in a sweatshirt. She placed them on Margarita's bed. "There they are," she said to Margarita, "Unwrap them and have a look. The engravings are on the bottom of each one."

"They **are** beautiful!" said Margarita after she had removed the sweatshirts and had stood the candlesticks up on her dresser. Just think, Tomás and Luisa used them in Spain 500 years ago and now they are sitting on my dresser in America, still beautiful and shiny."

"My grandmother thinks they may have been a wedding present to Tomás and Luisa.

They are shiny only because my grandmother insisted on polishing them just before I packed them. They actually were very tarnished before that. I wish there was some way we could find out who else has used them," said Bonnie.

"My great aunt Laura is very old," said Margarita. "She remembers her grandmother, Ana, who told her that she remembered seeing the candlesticks being used once when she was a young girl in Mexico. We can ask Aunt Laura more when we see her tomorrow. I know she'll love seeing the candlesticks."

✺　　　✺　　　✺

Bonnie and Margarita were sitting in the back of Margarita's family car heading down California Route #5 from San Francisco to Los Angeles. Margarita's mother was driving.

"You'll love Great Aunt Laura," said Margarita to Bonnie. "She's a lot of fun. I'm so glad you could come to California this summer."

"I'm glad, too. I really wanted to meet you," said Bonnie. "Also because it's always so hot in Tucson in the summer. I usually go to Albuquerque to stay with my grandmother during August, but this year my brother, Juan, wanted to go there. My mother said that since it really was his turn to go to Albuquerque, I could visit you as long as I had enough money to pay for the bus. So here I am! Your Aunt Laura wrote to me, too. She also told me about her urn. She sounds real nice."

"Here we are, girls," said Margarita's mother, as she stopped the car in front of a small, but very nice looking house. It was on a quiet curvy street lined with trees on both sides. Bonnie could see oranges and grapefruits hanging from the branches of the trees. "Aunt Laura must have kept Jumpy inside this morning so you two can go on up and ring the bell," said Margarita's mother.

After Margarita rang the doorbell, Bonnie heard bouncing and scratching noises coming from the inside of the front door, and loud deep barks. A tall clay urn stood to the right of the front door. Bonnie asked Margarita, "Is this the urn your aunt told me about?"

"Yes, Bonnie, it is beautiful." commented Margarita.

"I love the flowers etched in the clay, don't you?" asked Bonnie.

Soon the door opened. Bonnie saw a wrinkled, grey haired, older woman who looked a lot like her own grandmother. She was holding tightly to a Black Lab's collar.

"Come in Margarita and Bonnie." She kissed each girl on her cheek. "I'm just making some chicken salad sandwiches in the kitchen for our lunch. I hope you will like it with chopped pecans and grapes. I'm trying out a new recipe. Margarita, is your mother coming in?" asked Aunt Laura as she led the girls into the kitchen.

"No, Aunt Laura. She promised Roberto that she would be back in time to watch at least part of his soccer game against Southside this afternoon. She said to tell you she will call you on Monday to make plans to come down to do some shopping and go out to lunch with you."

"Too bad, I was hoping to see her today. But, never mind, we'll have a nice lunch anyway. I've cleaned off the table on the patio in back. Margarita, will you take that plate of sandwiches outside please?"

"Sure, Aunt Laura." Margarita picked up the plate and went out the back door.

"Bonnie, please take out the napkins, glasses and the pitcher of lemonade."

"Sure, Aunt Laura, I love lemonade!"

"Then you'll really love this lemonade. I made it out of lemons that I picked from my tree in the back yard just this morning!"

The three sat down around the table on the patio. Jumpy was running around the fenced in back yard.

"How do you like the chicken salad with the grapes and pecans?" asked Aunt Laura.

"I love it!" said Margarita.

"So do I!" said Bonnie.

"The recipe was in *The L.A. Times* yesterday. I wanted to try something a little different. Chicken salad can be so boring. I like it, too. I think I'll make some for my bridge group next month. Bonnie, did you see the urn outside the front door?" asked Aunt Laura.

"Yes, I did. I think it's beautiful, but I didn't see the magic part that you touch for good luck. I would like to take a closer look."

Aunt Laura wiped her mouth with her napkin. "As soon as you girls finish eating we'll go around to the front. I'll show you the worn area of the urn that I touch and that many have touched before me."

When Bonnie and Margarita had finished eating, all three went back into the house and out the front door. Aunt Laura lifted the urn carefully and placed it on the front walk where they all could stand around it.

Aunt Laura stooped over and pointed to a place near the base of the urn.

"Look here, Bonnie. Can you see where a square piece of clay looks as if it had been added to the rest of the urn?"

"Yes, I see it, Aunt Laura."

"Now lean down and touch it lightly with your fingers," she instructed the girls.

"Ooh, it feels as smooth as silk," said Bonnie as she rubbed her fingers back and forth over the spot that Aunt Laura had pointed out.

Suddenly they heard barking and saw that Jumpy was running toward them at a very fast clip. He was heading directly toward the urn.

"Stop, Jumpy!" Aunt Laura shouted as she ran to catch hold of his collar.

But she was too late. Jumpy dodged Aunt Laura and kept running. He ran right into the urn and knocked it over onto the cement walk. The urn shattered into small shards of clay that scattered along the walk.

"Bad dog!" said Aunt Laura as she slapped Jumpy's rear end. "I didn't know you could jump over the fence. Now I can't trust you in the back yard without a leash! I guess it's silly of me to get so mad at Jumpy. He couldn't know how much I valued that old urn. Really I should have kept him tied up even if the back yard is fenced in. I will from now on. But the damage has been done! I can't do anything about it now. Doesn't the front door look bare without the urn standing next to it? I am going to miss seeing my urn there and even more I will miss my rubbing it whenever I pass it. I hope bad things won't start happening to me or our family. I thought of my parents whenever I touched the urn. They have been gone a long time, but I still miss them a lot. The urn always felt like my link to them. It never occurred to me that the urn would be gone someday, too. But I can't really blame Jumpy. He just wanted to be where we were.

I blame myself for not taking more precautions to protect the urn. I feel just awful."

"What's that?" Margarita asked as she bent down and picked up an oblong shard that looked bigger than all the rest. "I think this was near the base. Maybe it's the magic amulet that keeps the evil spirits away. Let's wash the clay off of it and see what it looks like." Margarita handed the oblong object to Aunt Laura.

"Aunt Laura, do you really believe in evil spirits?" asked Bonnie.

"No, Bonnie, but, I celebrated my 90th birthday last week. I have led a fortunate life. I haven't been sick a day except for an occasional cold or flu. I can't prove that is because of the urn, but I have never ignored it since I was a little girl. I did then, what I saw my parents do. By the time I was an adult, touching the urn had become a habit. I could see no reason to stop doing it."

"Did your parents believe in evil spirits?" asked Bonnie.

"Oh, yes they did! They were sure something bad would happen to them if they walked into or out of the house without touching the urn."

Aunt Laura and the girls took the oblong shard into the kitchen. First they knocked off whatever hardened clay they could with the back of a knife, then Aunt Laura held it under the faucet and started washing off the thin layer of clay that was still on it. What emerged looked like a small rectangular silver box. When it was all cleaned off they noticed that there was a symbol engraved on the front. It looked like a curved line with three wavy vertical lines pointing up, a little like a wavy three-tined fork. Aunt Laura got some silver polish and polished the little box until it was shiny and beautiful.

"Hmm," said Aunt Laura as she held the silver box up to the light coming through the window. "I could be wrong, but I think I've seen this symbol somewhere before. But where? It looks a little familiar, but I don't know where I've seen it. Ummm. Ooh, now I think I know. I think it may be the Hebrew letter that I always see in front of the synagogue in Inglewood when I take Jumpy for a walk. I know how we'll find out. I'll ask Rabbi Jacobson who lives down the street. He owns a black Lab also, and I've become a little friendly with him when we meet while walking the dogs. I'm sure he'll be glad to help us. I'll call him up and see if he'll be home this afternoon.

⁂

Later that afternoon, Aunt Laura handed the silver box to Rabbi Jacobson. She and the two girls were sitting in the chairs facing the Rabbi's desk in his study.

"You are very observant, Mrs. Perez to recognize this symbol as a Hebrew letter," said Rabbi Jacobson. "It is called a 'Shin' and is the first letter in the Hebrew word, 'Shalom'. Many congregations have this word meaning 'peace' as part of their names. The 'Shin' on this box, however does not stand for 'Shalom.' It represents 'Shaddai', which is one of the names of 'God'. Jewish people never spell out the word 'God'. Different words or acronyms are used to represent the name of God. "Shaddai' is used on little cases like this one that you have found hidden in your urn. It is called a 'Mezuza'. It contains a small scroll of parchment on which the 'Shema' prayer has been hand written by a professional scribe. The 'Shema' is the most important of all Jewish prayers. For this reason Jews have placed the scroll in cases made of silver and many other durable materials and have always attached the cases to the doorposts of their homes as it is commanded in the 'Shema' prayer. Jewish people touch the Mezuza with their fingers and kiss their fingers whenever they walk past the Mezuza.

Its purpose is to remind them to behave according to the Laws of Moses when they are in their homes and also when they leave their homes."

"But why was this Mezuza, if that's what it is, hidden in the urn belonging to a Catholic like me?" asked Aunt Laura.

"You ask a very good question, Mrs. Perez and if you have the time I can tell you a long story that I think will answer that question."

"We have plenty of time," said Aunt Laura, "and we're very interested to hear the story."

"Does the date 1492 mean anything to you?" asked Rabbi Jacobson.

Aunt Laura answered, "Of course it does. That's the date we learned in school that Christopher Columbus discovered America."

"You're right, of course, but most schools don't teach another set of events that happened in Spain during that same year. When King Ferdinand and Queen Isabela became the rulers of Spain in 1492, they decided that every Spanish citizen must be Catholic. They told all the Jews there that they had to leave Spain or convert to Catholicism."

"I just thought of another verse to the old poem," said Bonnie: "In 1492, Columbus sailed the ocean blue, in 1492, in Spain, it was a sin to be a Jew."

Rabbi Jacobson continued, "Many Jewish people left. They went to Holland or Africa or Portugal, but, many had no place to go. Soon all countries closed their doors to more Jewish immigration. Those who could not leave converted in order to stay alive. Queen Isabela and King Ferdinand imposed horrible punishments on everyone, even the 'old' Catholics who they thought did not fulfill all of their obligations as good Catholics. This became known as the 'Spanish Inquisition'. Catholics who did not go to Mass regularly or to confession or disrespected the Catholic church in other ways were put to death by being burned alive in a public ceremony. Many Jews converted wholeheartedly, but others only acted outwardly as Catholics and continued to perform their Jewish rituals and prayers in their homes. The priests ordered everyone to report to them the names of all 'New' Christians who they suspected still performed Jewish rituals in secret. Those reported were also arrested and then burned to death. As you can imagine, those performing Jewish rituals went to great lengths to keep them secret. If they were used to having a Mezuza on their doorposts, they would hide it somehow so it could not be seen. I even heard that some had ceramic Madonna statues made with a special compartment that could hold the Mezuza. They placed these Madonnas near the front door, where the family could touch the place where the Mezuza was hidden as they entered and left their homes. After Columbus discovered America, many Jews came to South America and Mexico on cargo ships to escape Ferdinand and Isabela's harsh rules and punishments. In Mexico, they could practice their religion in the open, at first, since the Indians there didn't care what religion the newcomers practiced. However, since Mexico was under Spanish rule, Queen Isabela soon decided that Mexico should be Catholic, too. She sent priests to Mexico to enforce Catholic belief throughout the country.

Those who wanted to observe their Jewish faith had to start doing so in secret again."

"Aunt Laura, our family is from Mexico, isn't it?" asked Bonnie.

"Yes, we are."

"Then maybe our ancestors were Jewish. That would answer your question about the Mezuza in your urn."

"And," added Margarita, "why we light candles in the cellar or other secret places."

Rabbi Jacobson continued, "Over the decades families continued to hold onto traditions even after they had forgotten their origin or their purpose."

"Thank you, Rabbi. That explains a lot of things that have been puzzling our families for years. Bonnie here, can be credited with pursuing answers to some of her questions. She has thus brought together members of our extended family who have never met, but follow similar rituals even though they don't know why. Bonnie wasn't satisfied with answers like, 'because we've always done it this way.' She owns some silver candlesticks that might give proof to what you have just told us. They are engraved 'Espana 1492.'"

Bonnie spoke up, interrupting Aunt Laura, "My grandmother asked me to light candles in them at sunset on Fridays to honor our ancestors and to keep our family free from evil spirits. She has lit them secretly in her pantry for many years. My mother refused to continue the tradition. When I turned twelve this fall, my grandmother asked me to carry on the tradition in our family. She believes she is the one who has kept our family safe since she faithfully lit the candles in her pantry each week since she was twelve. She gave me a diary in which her mother, my great grandmother, Ester, wrote about the secret rituals she followed, but didn't understand."

"Very interesting! I'd like to see those candlesticks and the diary. I might be able to explain some things to you that your great grandmother mentions. Jewish people light candles at sunset on Fridays not to keep away evil spirits, Bonnie, but to welcome the Sabbath, which we celebrate on Saturday.

Bonnie, did your grandmother teach you the prayer to say while you light the candles?" asked Rabbi Jacobson.

"No, Rabbi, but when I discovered her lighting the candles in her pantry she was saying two words, 'boruch atta' and 'ah-doe-nigh.'"

"I just explained to you that 'Shema' is the name of our most important prayer. It is recited at every Jewish service. 'Adonai' is one of the words we use when we refer to God. I assume these are the words your ancestors remembered, when they forgot the prayers in their entirety over the years. If you would like to learn more about what I think was your ancestors' faith, you can sit in on the conversion classes that I teach every summer once a week from July 1 to Labor Day."

"I would like to learn more, but if I do go to the class, do I have to convert to Judaism?" asked Bonnie.

"No, of course not!" said Rabbi Jacobson. "You were baptized when you were a little baby. And I'm sure you feel comfortable with the faith your parents have taught you. At some later time once you have learned more of what I believe may be the faith of your ancestors you might want to think again about conversion."

"Rabbi, your classes sound interesting to me," said Aunt Laura, "but at my age I know that I want to end my life as a Catholic, just as I have lived it. When my time comes I want Father Michael from St. Sofia's to hear my final confession and give me the last rites and a Catholic burial."

"I understand, Mrs. Perez," said Rabbi Jacobson. "Does Father Michael know of your wishes?"

"I'll talk to him next Sunday when I go to Mass," said Aunt Laura. "By the way, girls, if the classes sound interesting to you, you both can stay here with me for the summer. Margarita knows that I have lots of room and extra beds. We could all go to the classes together! I think that would be fun! But now it's time for us to go home and let the rabbi work on his sermon. We have bothered him long enough!"

"No bother, I loved seeing your hidden treasure! Say hello to Jumpy!" said Rabbi Jacobson as he reached for a book in the bookcase in back of his desk.

As they were walking home, Aunt Laura spoke to Margarita and Bonnie. "I'm not sure the rest of the family needs all this information. Some may become very upset. Let's keep it under our hats for a while, at least until we understand more ourselves."

"Good idea," said Margarita.

"I will have to tell my mother," said Bonnie, "so she will let me come to L.A. again next summer. I think she'll be happy to know that 'evil spirits' are not lurking around our house just because she refused to do the candle lighting. By the way Aunt Laura, I brought the silver candlesticks with me. Would you like to see them?"

"Of course I would. Maybe later on, after dinner, we could light the candles. Sunset is very late these long summer days."

"Do you think we should light the candles now that we know that it is a Jewish tradition and we're not Jews?" asked Bonnie.

"I would like to continue my family's tradition anyway. What harm can it do?" answered Aunt Laura.

Margarita said, "I would like to see the candles lit in those beautiful silver candlesticks."

"All right, let's do it. Where's your secret closet? And where are the candles?" asked Bonnie.

"Wait a minute, Bonnie, we haven't had dinner yet. What would you girls like to have tonight?"

"How about pizza," Margarita suggested.

"That's a good idea. I'll call my favorite place. It's just a few blocks away. They'll deliver it in no time."

After they walked into Aunt Laura's house, Laura went right to the telephone to order the pizza. A half hour later the doorbell rang and the pizza was delivered. They took it out back to eat on the patio again.

"Aunt Laura, have you always lit your candles in a secret place, also?" asked Bonnie.

"Yes, Bonnie. I have a big pantry off my kitchen. I keep the candles in there and I go in there to light them. But now we don't have to do this in secret anymore after Rabbi Jacobson's explanation. So let's light them right in the living room tonight."

"That will seem very odd to me since I'm used to doing it in the cellar," said Margarita. "But I'll be happy to do it in the living room with you. Bonnie, where did you put the candlesticks?"

"I think I put them down in the kitchen. I'll go get them."

She walked into the kitchen and picked up the totebag that she had put them in when she left Margarita's house. When Bonnie took them out of the totebag she took the sweatshirts off of them. Then she carefully put them on the coffee table in the living room. Aunt Laura went into the pantry to get the candles and matches. When Aunt Laura returned she placed the candles into the silver candlesticks, but first she turned the candlesticks over to read the inscriptions on the bottom.

"We are really fortunate," she said, "to have these beautiful old candlesticks. Everyone in our family who used them had to really take good care of them. They still look beautiful."

Laura had also brought a little tray from the pantry to put under the candlesticks so the coffee table wouldn't get scratched, or splattered with hot wax. Bonnie lit the match and then lit the two candles. Then she covered her eyes. Margarita said, "Boruch atta ah-doe-nigh..." Then, Aunt Laura said, "Amen." Afterwards, Aunt Laura took the hands of Margarita and Bonnie in hers. "I feel especially close to you girls tonight." She kissed them both on their cheeks. The three stood around the coffee table in a little circle, holding hands.

"Aunt Laura," said Margarita. "Maybe Jumpy did us a favor when he broke the urn. I will miss seeing it by your door, but I am happy to not have to worry about keeping things secret anymore. I really hated going down to the cellar every week. I'm looking forward to learning about the Jewish religion, especially if it meant so much to our ancestors that they held on to its beliefs when they could all have been killed because of it."

"I'm sure some were killed, but many survived," said Aunt Laura. "I can't imagine what I would do if some powerful person told me that I couldn't worship God as a Catholic anymore. This would never happen in the United States, because our country was founded on the principle of freedom of religion. Unfortunately the Jewish people have often had to suffer over many centuries in many lands so that they could hold on to their beliefs. I also look forward to learning more about their, or, are they 'our' beliefs next summer."

Just then the doorbell rang. "Now who could that be?" asked Aunt Laura as she hurried to the front door. She grabbed Jumpy's collar with her left hand. He was already jumping up and scratching at the door. With her right hand Laura turned the knob and opened the door.

"Excuse us for disturbing you at this late hour, Mrs. Perez. We were just walking home from services and saw that your living room lights were still on," Rabbi Jacobson said. "I think you know that my wife is an antique collector. She very much wanted to see your candlesticks. I hope it isn't too late to let us have a quick look at them. Ah, there they are! I see you lit them in here tonight."

"Mrs. Perez, they are beautiful!" said Mrs. Jacobson. "Could I stop in tomorrow morning when the candles are no longer burning to look at the inscriptions on the bottoms?"

"Of course you can. I'll be interested to hear what you can tell us about them. The girls will be picked up around nine, and I know that Bonnie will want to take them back to Tucson, so come over before nine," said Aunt Laura.

"Thank you, I'll be here by eight-thirty."

"Girls, maybe it's time to go to bed since you have to get up so early," said Aunt Laura.

"All right Aunt Laura, we'll go right up," answered Margarita.

✺ ✺ ✺

The girls headed upstairs, talking and laughing as they went.

"To tell you the truth," said Bonnie to Margarita, "I never really did believe in evil spirits."

"Neither did I," said Margarita.

Then both girls started to laugh. At the top of the steps they shouted, "Good night, Aunt Laura. See you in the morning. Shalom!" Then they started laughing again as they headed to their rooms.

II

Some Bad News

When Bonnie and Margarita returned to San Francisco, there was a phone call for Bonnie from her mother, telling her that she must come home right away. Her grandmother had died and the family was flying to Mexico for the funeral the next day.

Mexico; The Present

Bonnie and her family gathered in a small circle around the coffin suspended over the open grave at the Santo Dominica cemetery. After the padre finished his prayers, the small group of relatives all crossed themselves as they said, "amen." As the coffin was being lowered into the ground, Bonnie wiped her eyes and stepped forward. She laid the white roses that she had bought at the airport in Mexico City on top of the coffin, then she turned away to walk along the path through the cemetery.

The path was shaded by lemon trees on both sides. She wanted to be alone to reminisce about her grandmother and mull over the new knowledge that she had learned about her family while in California with Margarita and Great Aunt Laura. She stopped in front of her great grandmother, Ester's, gravestone. As she gazed at it she remembered the diary that Ester had begun when she was 12 and how she had to start lighting the candles in secret. She remembered reading how confused and troubled Ester had been learning about her family's deep secrets. "If only you were still alive," Bonnie said aloud to the gravestone, "I could explain to you everything that I learned in L.A! I wonder if you would really want to know the facts about the candles and the need for secrecy." Probably not, Bonnie thought.

Bonnie felt the pressure of a hand on her shoulder. She turned and saw her mother. Oh, no, she thought, I guess that's the end of my solitary walk!

"Were you talking to the gravestone?" Mother asked. "I thought that I heard you mumbling something."

"No, you must be hearing things," Bonnie lied. "Why would I talk to a gravestone?"

"Well, people do talk to gravestones sometimes for many different reasons. They may ask for forgiveness for some thing that happened in the past or, just to say 'I miss you.'"

"Why would I do that?" asked Bonnie. "She died before I was even born."

"That's right. I was pregnant with you when I came to Ester's burial with my mother. At that time my mother showed me a few other graves belonging to members of our family. There is one that I would like to show you... Follow me.

Bonnie's mother started walking down the path. Bonnie turned and followed her. After walking about 10 minutes Bonnie's mother slowed down, then stopped to pull up a tall weed which was hiding the inscription on a small gravestone. With the weed gone Bonnie read:

Bonita Sanchez 10, Abril. 1776. – 19 Mayo. 1835.

The rest of the gravestone was etched with flowers. As Bonnie stared at it, she noticed something else unusual about it. It had no cross on it! All of the other gravestones in this Catholic cemetery had crosses on them.

As Bonnie's mother circled the gravestone, continuing to pull up weeds, she told Bonnie, "When I first saw this gravestone I got the idea to name the baby that I was carrying, 'Bonnie' if she was a girl. My mother thought it was a wonderful idea to memorialize one of our ancestors. I just thought it was a pretty name. That's why I wanted to show you this gravestone."

"Thanks Mom, I like my name, too. I'm happy to see the grave of my ancestor and namesake! Did you notice that it's the only gravestone in this whole cemetery without a cross? I learned something while visiting in Los Angeles that might explain the reason. Bonnie told her mother what she had learned from Rabbi Jacobson and asked whether she could return to California the next summer to learn more about Judaism.

"Yes, you may go, I'm happy that you had a good time with your cousin and her great aunt. But, don't forget you were brought up to be a Catholic. I hope that the rabbi won't expect you to convert if you take his classes.

"He won't. Aunt Laura wants to take his classes too and she already told him she wants to remain Catholic and have a Catholic funeral when she dies. He said he understood her thinking and agreed with her. I think that Bonita may have known of her Jewish heritage because I was studying the flowers on the gravestone while you were walking around it pulling up weeds. I noticed that flower on the lower left has an unusual looking stamen." Bonnie pointed to the flower. "See that stamen. It looks like a three tined fork. That's kind of what the Hebrew letter on top of the silver box looked like. It is a symbol that means God in Hebrew. I think that symbol hidden in the flower, plus the fact that there is no cross on this gravestone means that Bonita, or whoever designed the stone, must have known she was Jewish.

"That's all very interesting," said Mother, "Now you're getting me intrigued. Maybe I'll try to learn more when I get back to Tucson. After all we have rabbis and synagogues in Tucson, too!

The End

Afterword

The inspiration for this young readers book occurred at my husband's hematology meeting in San Antonio in the early 1990s where we attended synagogue services one Friday night. The program included interviews of a young Catholic couple who had gradually come to realize that their families must have been secret Jews. I began to study this phenomenon and soon attended a conference on hidden Jews of the Southwest held in Albuquerque and directed by Dr. Stanley Hordes. Research followed and the idea of writing a novel about a converso family germinated. A major source of information was David M. Gitlitz' book, *Secrecy And Deceit. The Religion Of The Crypto-Jews.*

–Vera W. Propp

Praise for
Candles in the Closet

"Vera Propp, former teacher, current author, demonstrates again in her most recent work, her sensitivity and skill in reaching the minds and hearts of young readers. "Candles in the Closet" tells of the flight of Conversos from Spain and Portugal to the New World in the 15th and 16th centuries and of their tenacity in secretly maintaining their faith and traditions despite dangers that beset them. The story of multiple generations is expertly told in language and settings that can be understood and appreciated by a wide range of readers. This book will be particularly meaningful to the millions of displaced persons who fled persecution in their countries of birth and found refuge and freedom to practice their faith in this country."

—Dvorah Heckelman,
Consultant to Partnership for Excellence in Jewish Education.

"Vera Propp gives us an intriguing journey through the Spanish Inquisition's inhuman persecution of Jews, including with a modern-day ending, complete with secret compartments, clandestine meetings, and closeted prayers. The reader will gain a whole new perspective on Columbus' voyage and its sponsors."

–Jim Trelease,
Author of *The Read-Aloud Handbook*